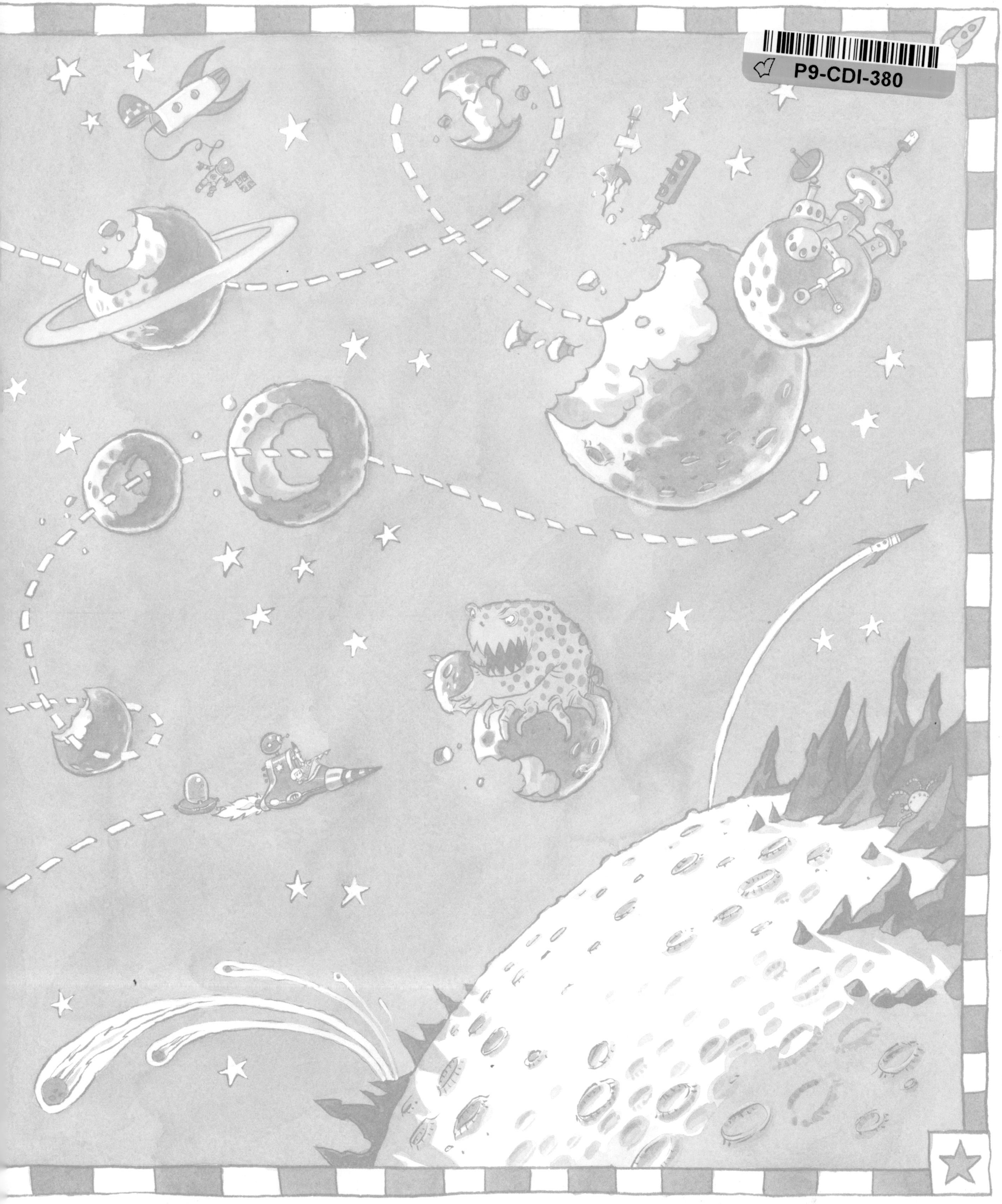

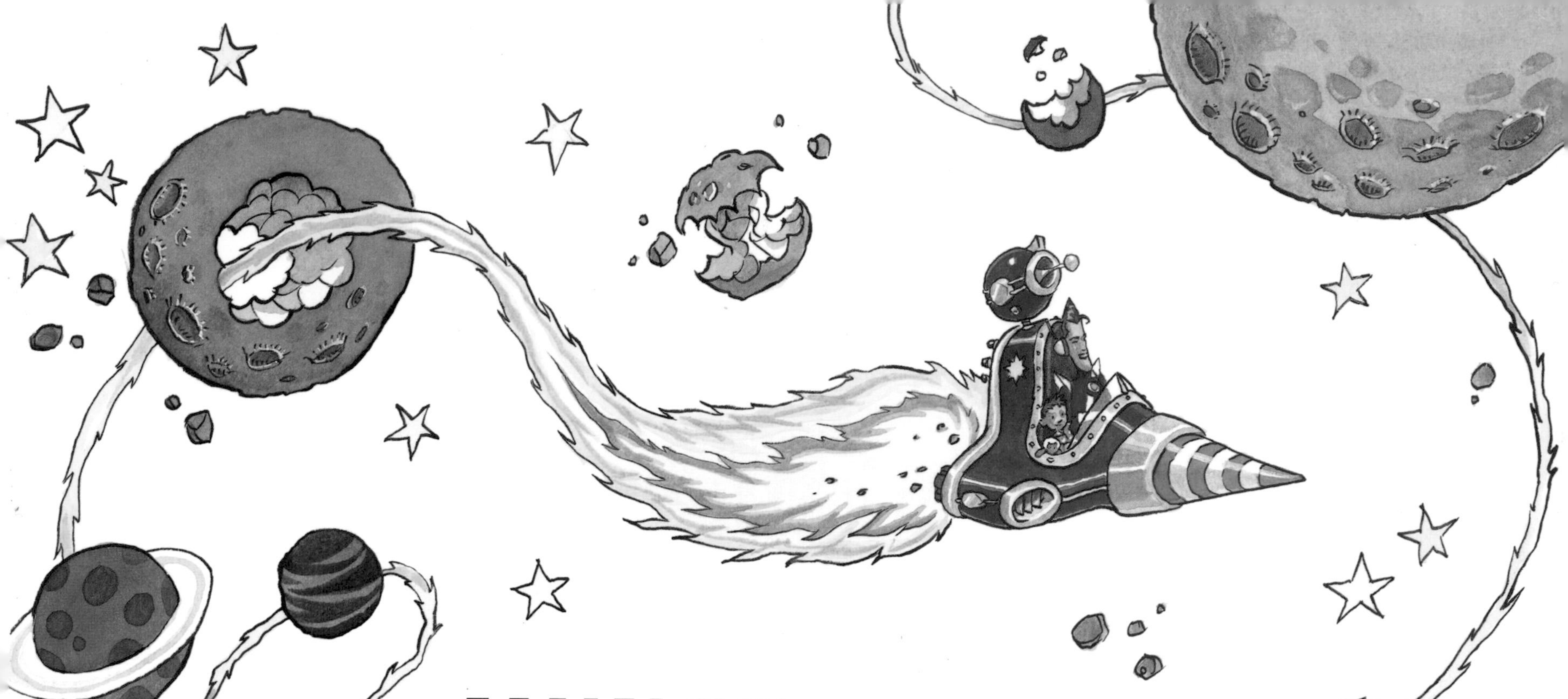

MUNGO AND THE SPIDERS FROM SPACE

by Timothy Knapman
illustrated by Adam Stower

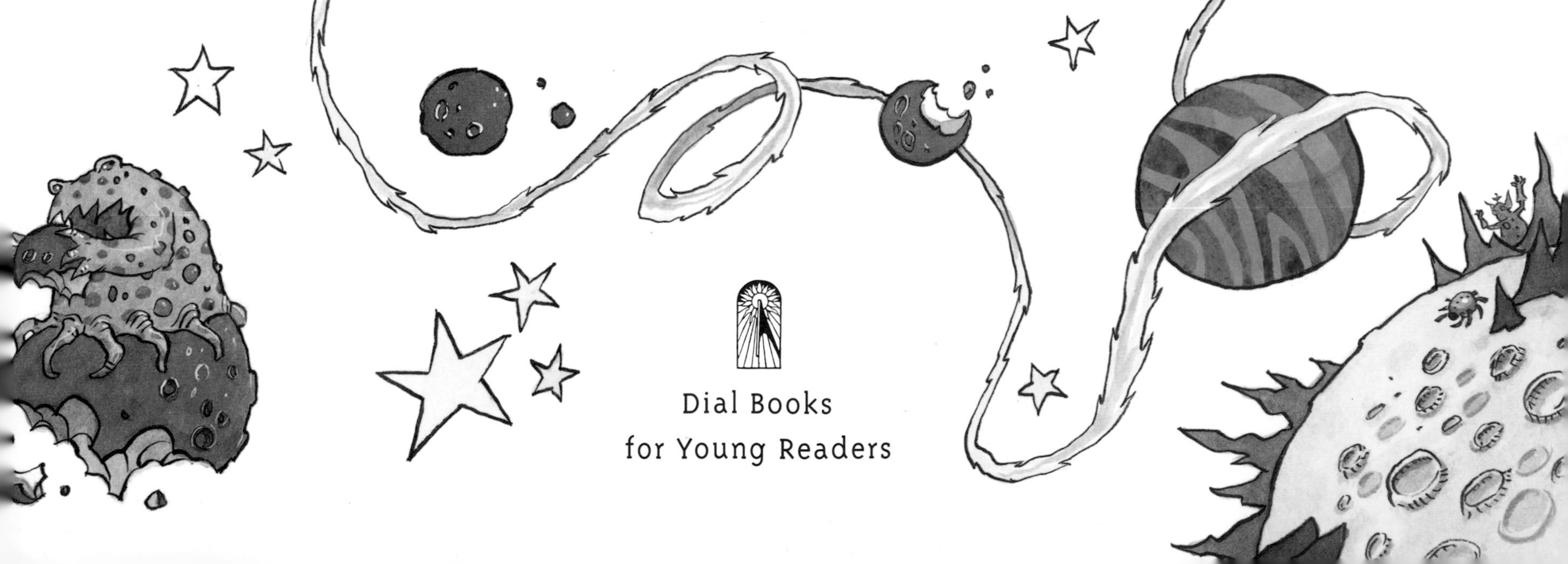

Dial Books
for Young Readers

This is Mungo.
He has just been given a book called
GALACTICUS AND GIZMO SAVE THE UNIVERSE!

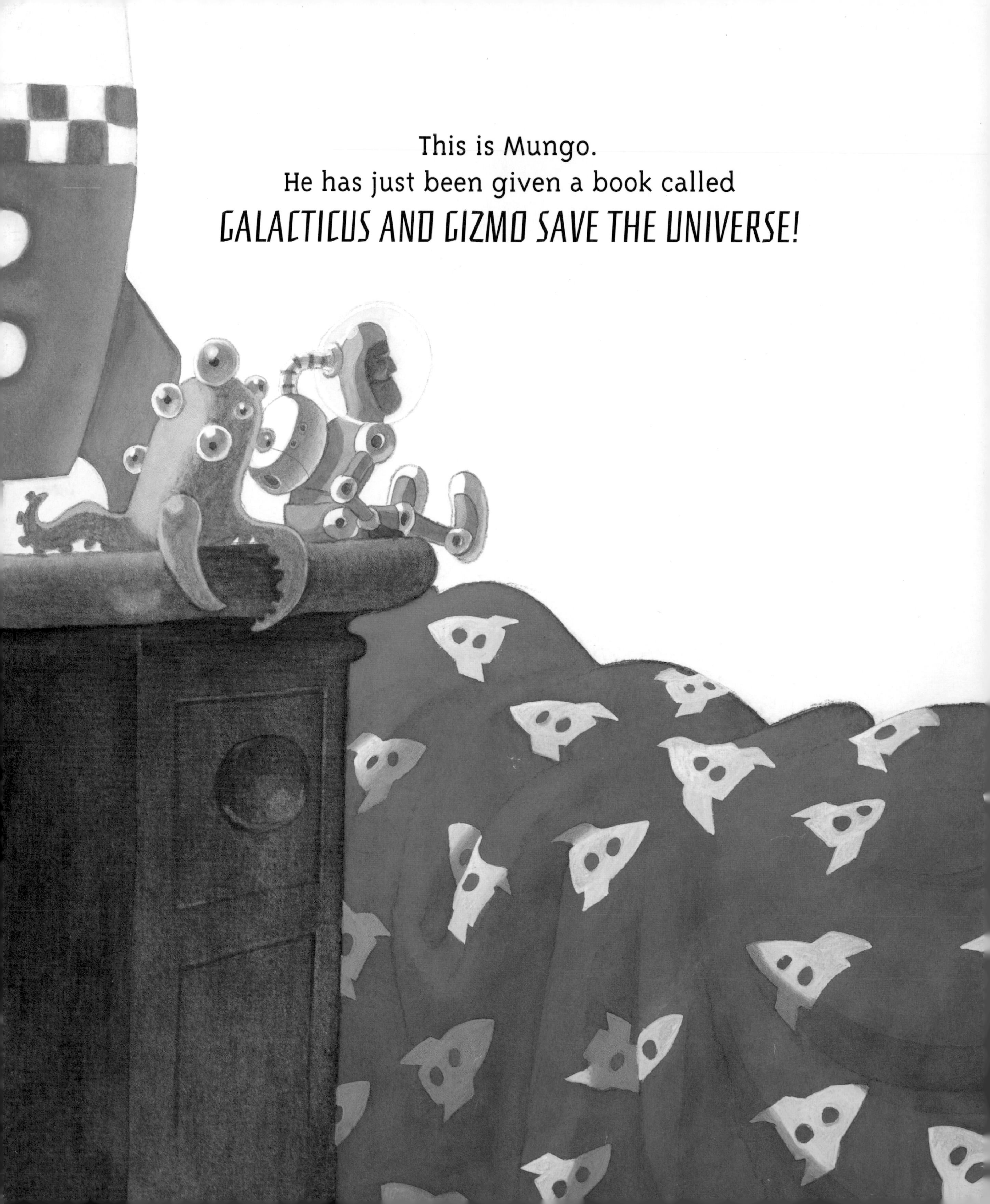

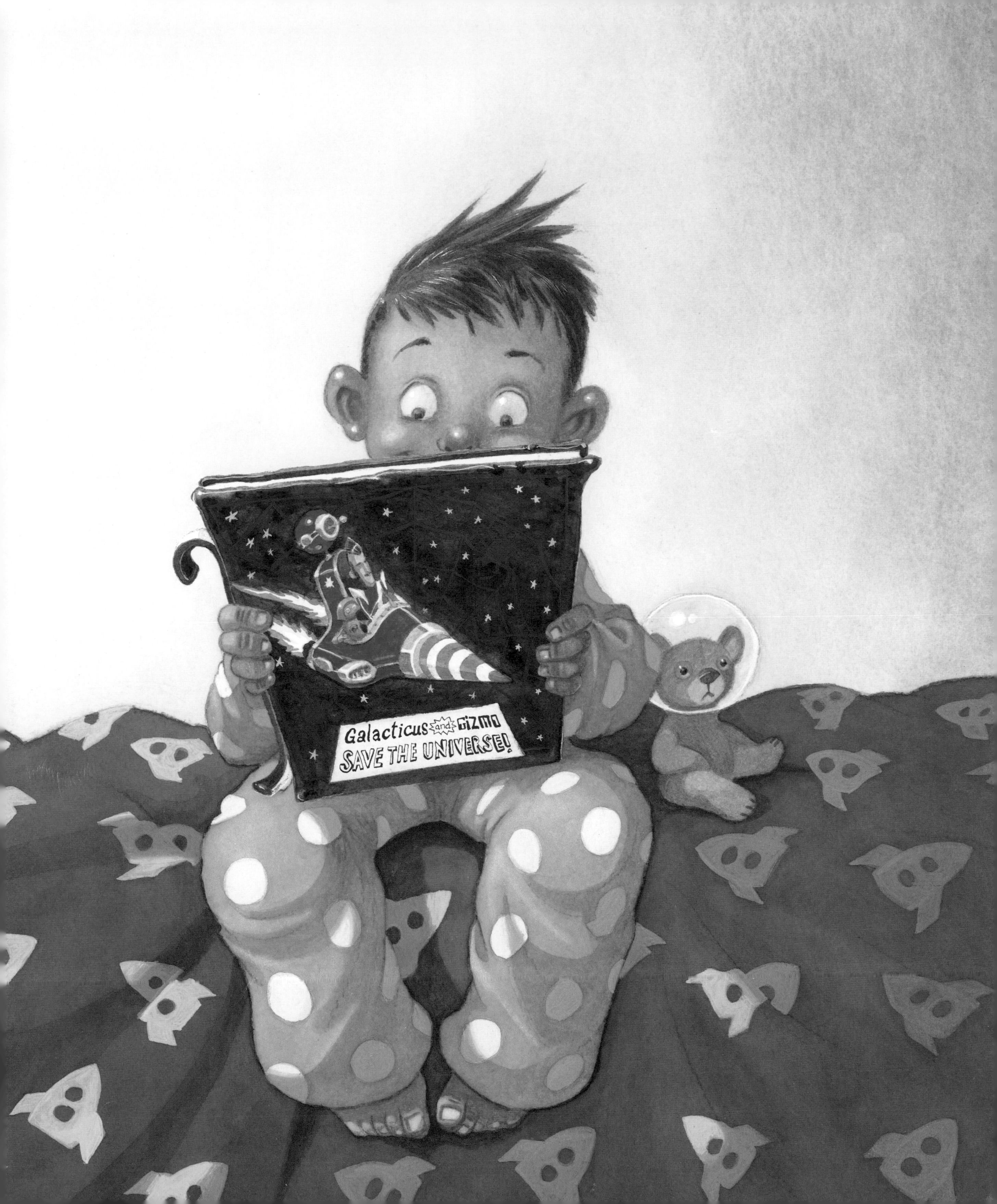
Galacticus and Gizmo
SAVE THE UNIVERSE!

His mom found it at a garage sale.
It was old and torn and tattered and stuck together with tape, but she knew Mungo would love it, just from the picture on the cover.

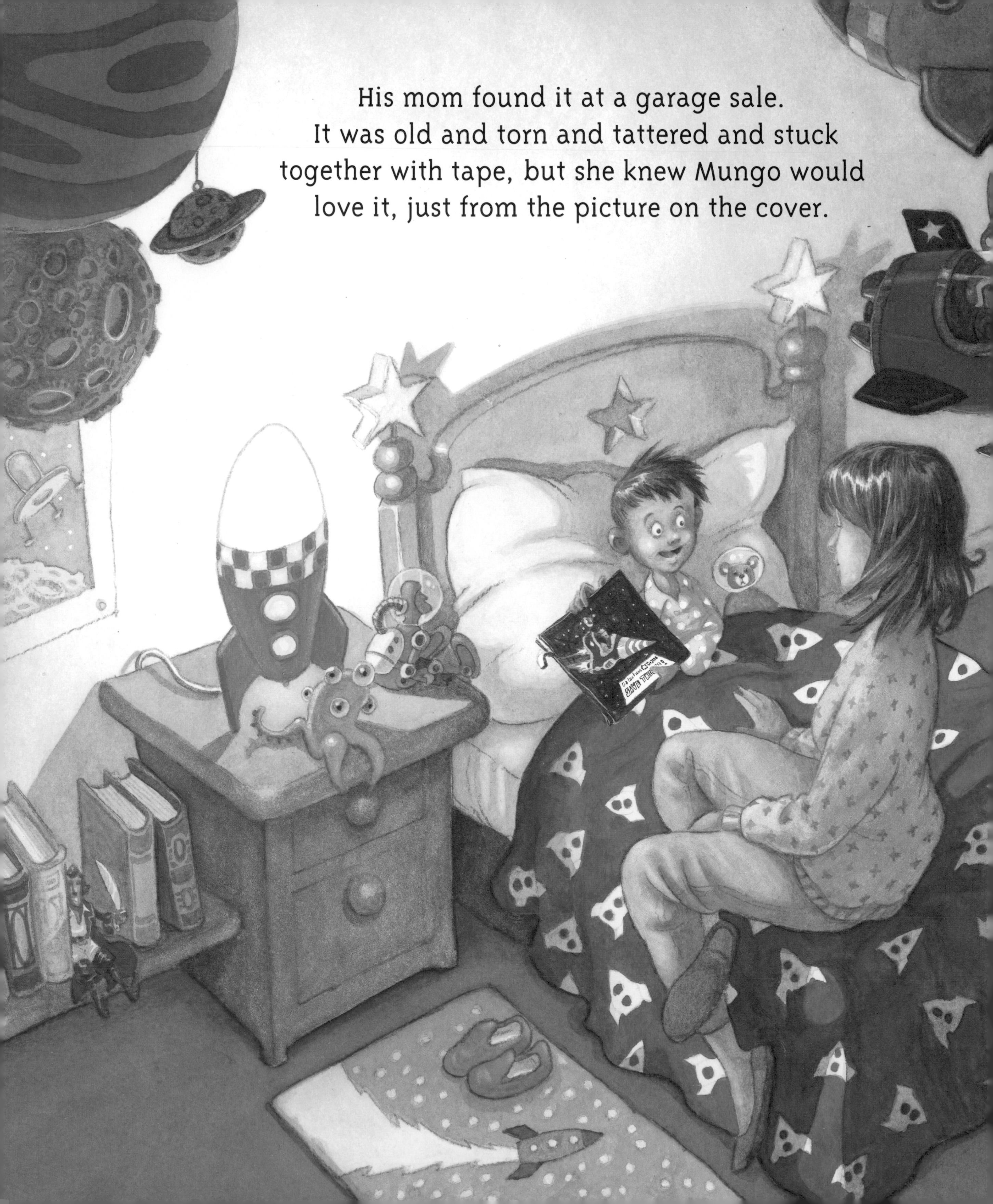

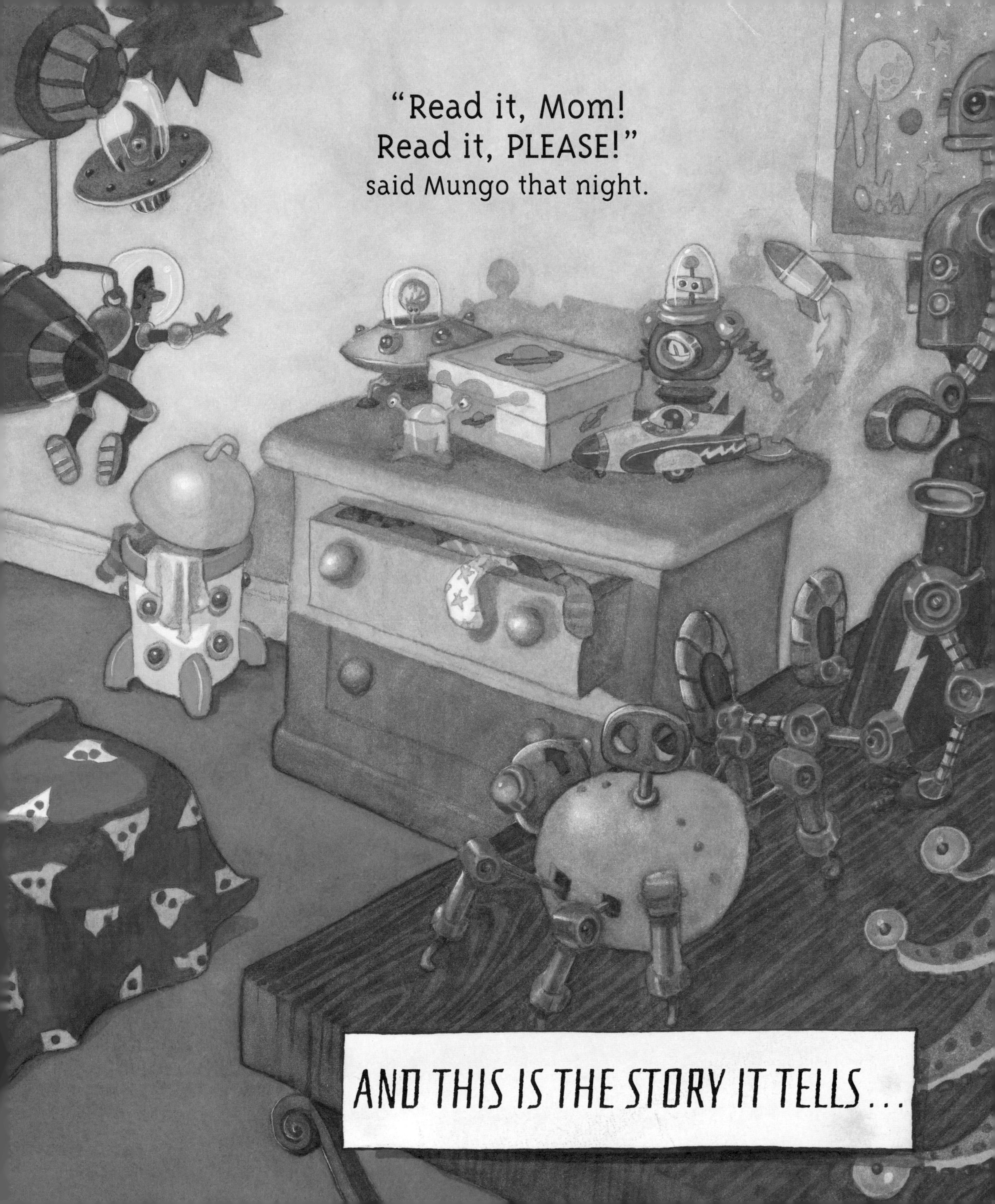

“Read it, Mom!
Read it, PLEASE!”
said Mungo that night.

AND THIS IS THE STORY IT TELLS . . .

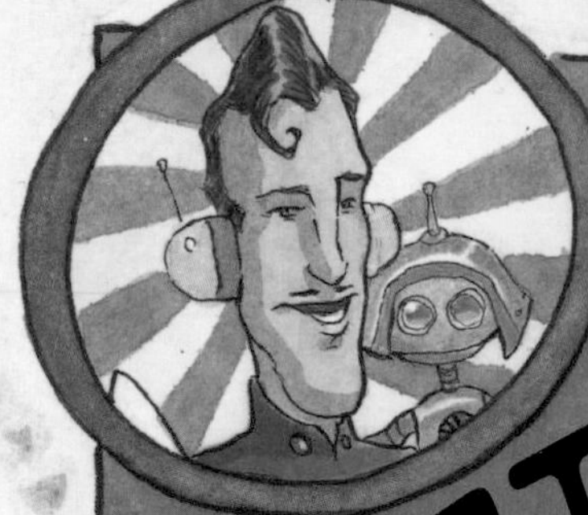

GALACTICUS and Gizmo

SAVE THE UNIVERSE!

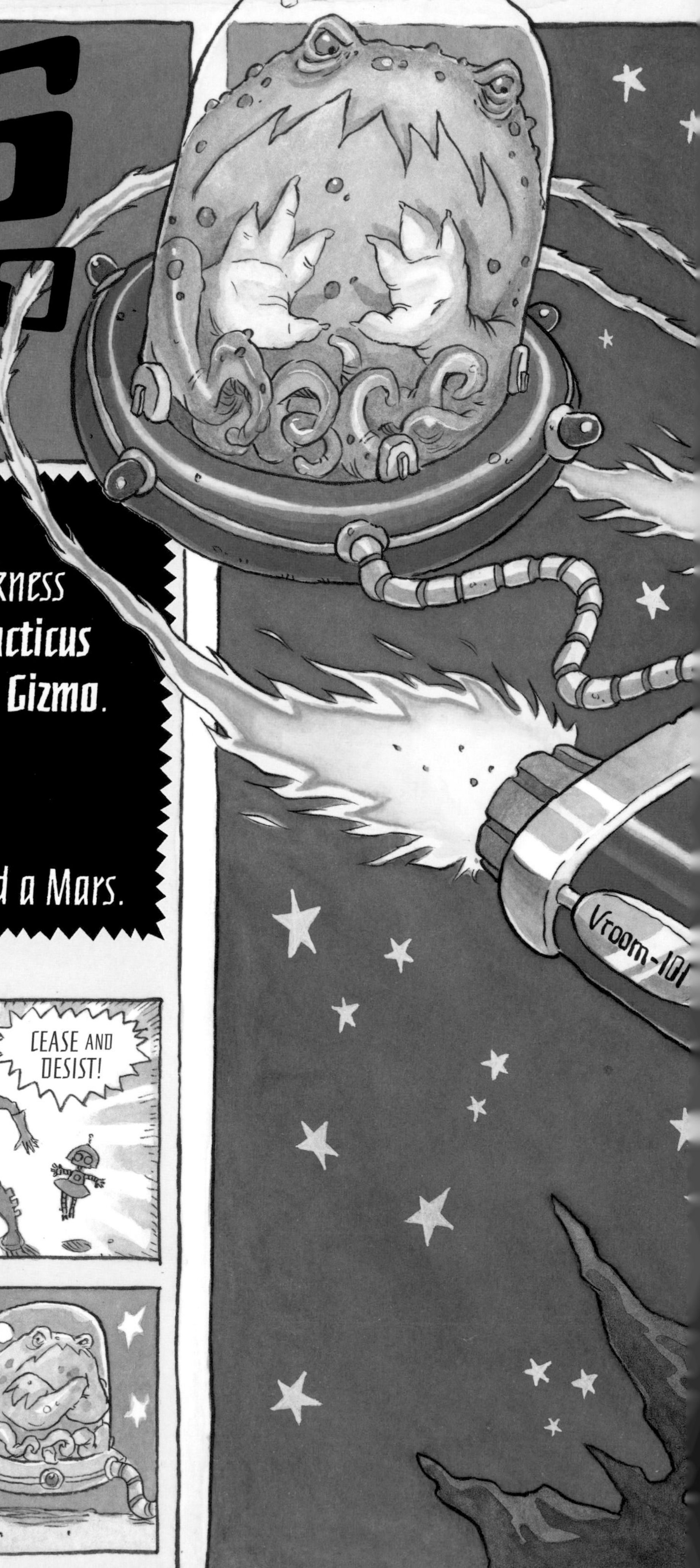

Vroom-101

The trusty rocket ship **Vroom-101** streaked across the winking, blinking blackness of space. AT THE CONTROLS: **Captain Galacticus of Star Squadron** and his sparky sidekick, **Gizmo**.

They were taking the **GNASHING, SLASHING GOBBLEBEAST** to space prison for eating two galaxies and a Mars.

OUR STORY SO FAR:

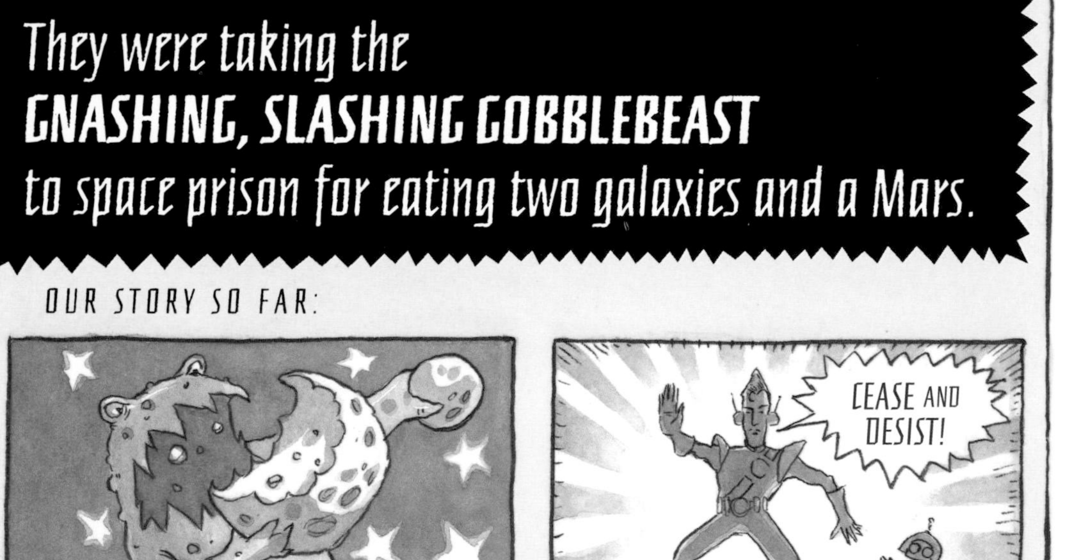

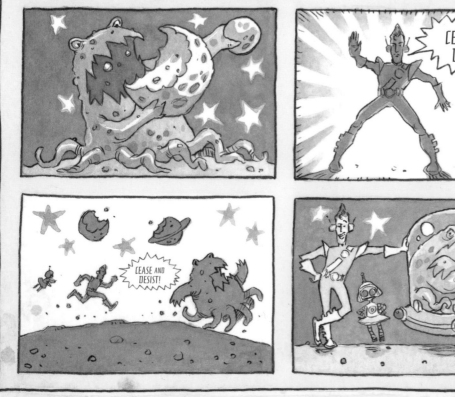

CEASE AND DESIST!
CEASE AND DESIST!

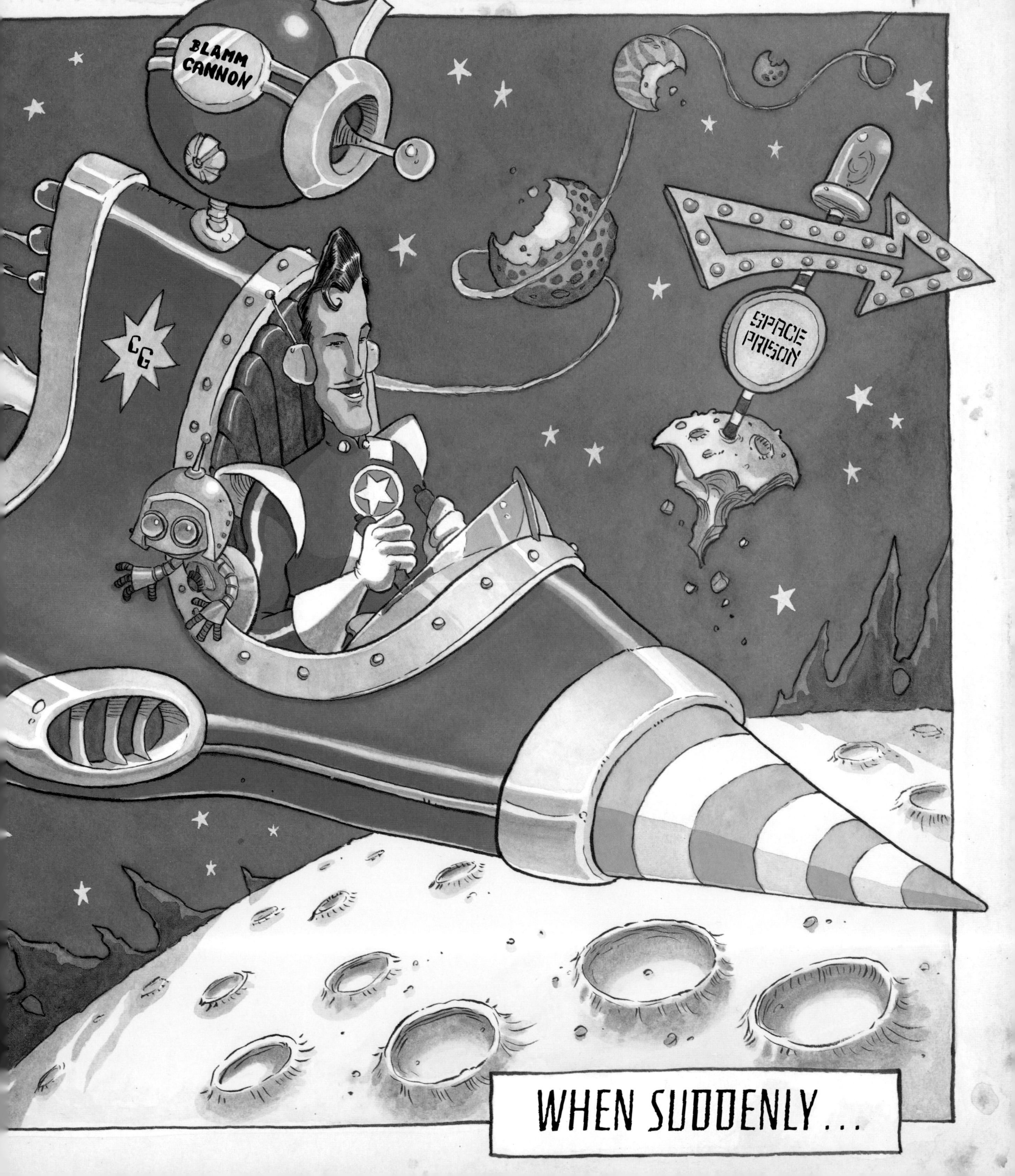
BLAMM CANNON
CG
SPACE PRISON
WHEN SUDDENLY . . .

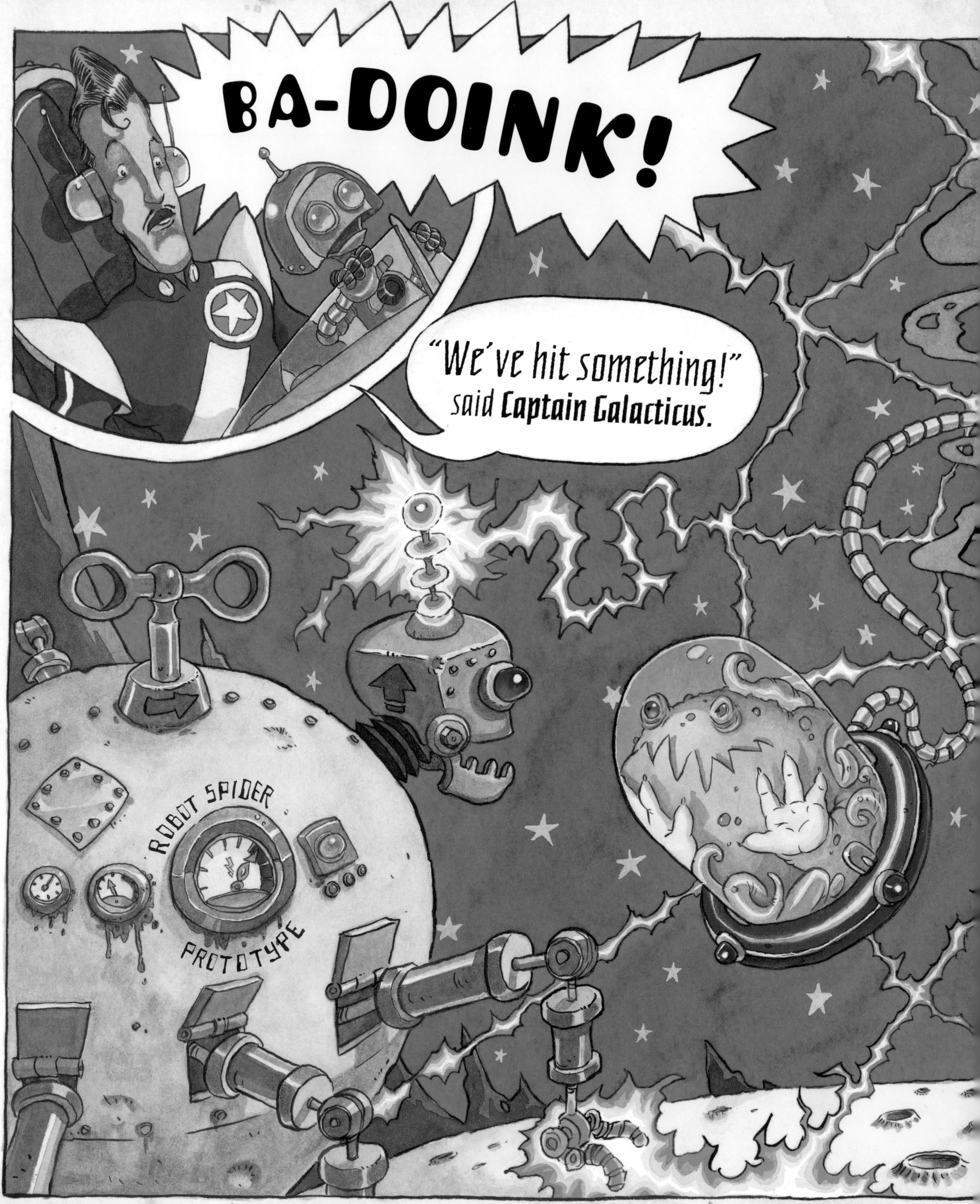
BA-DOINK!
"We've hit something!" said Captain Galacticus.
ROBOT SPIDER PROTOTYPE

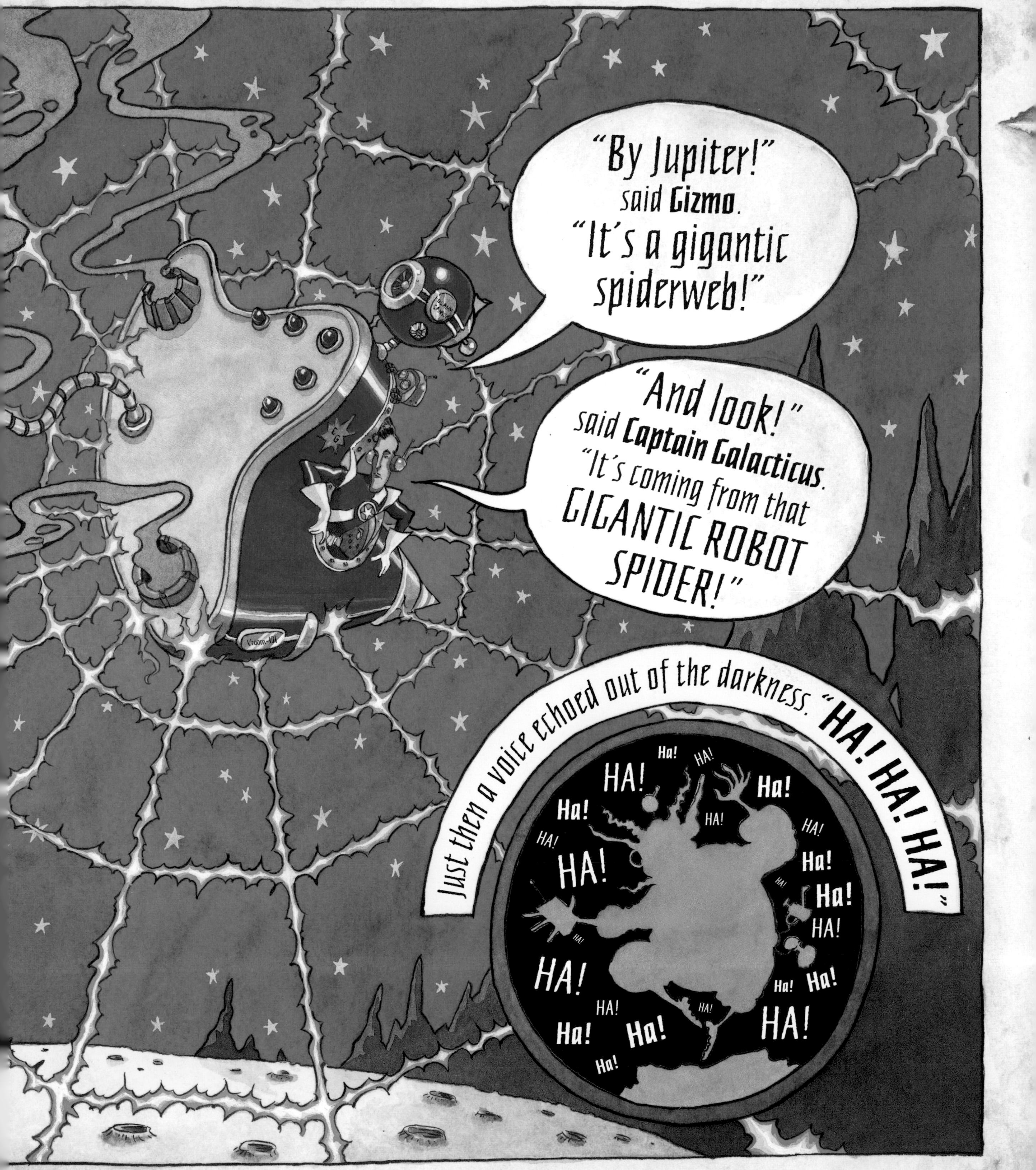
"By Jupiter!" said Gizmo. "It's a gigantic spiderweb!"
"And look!" said Captain Galacticus. "It's coming from that GIGANTIC ROBOT SPIDER!"
Just then a voice echoed out of the darkness. "HA! HA! HA!"
HA! Ha! HA! Ha! HA! Ha! HA! HA! Ha! HA! Ha! HA! HA! Ha! HA! Ha! Ha! HA! Ha! Ha! HA! HA! Ha!

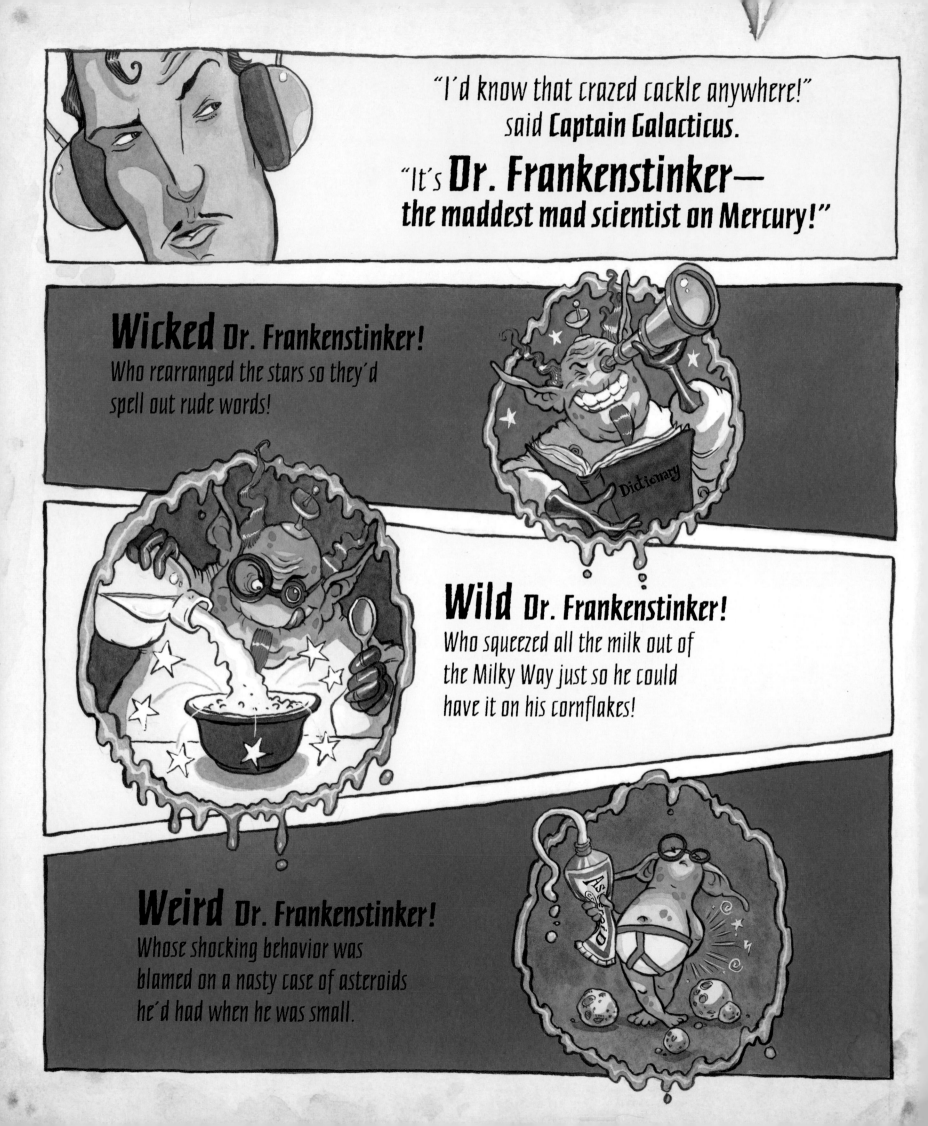

"I'd know that crazed cackle anywhere!"
said **Captain Galacticus.**

"It's **Dr. Frankenstinker—**
the maddest mad scientist on Mercury!"

Wicked Dr. Frankenstinker!
Who rearranged the stars so they'd
spell out rude words!

Wild Dr. Frankenstinker!
Who squeezed all the milk out of
the Milky Way just so he could
have it on his cornflakes!

Weird Dr. Frankenstinker!
Whose shocking behavior was
blamed on a nasty case of asteroids
he'd had when he was small.

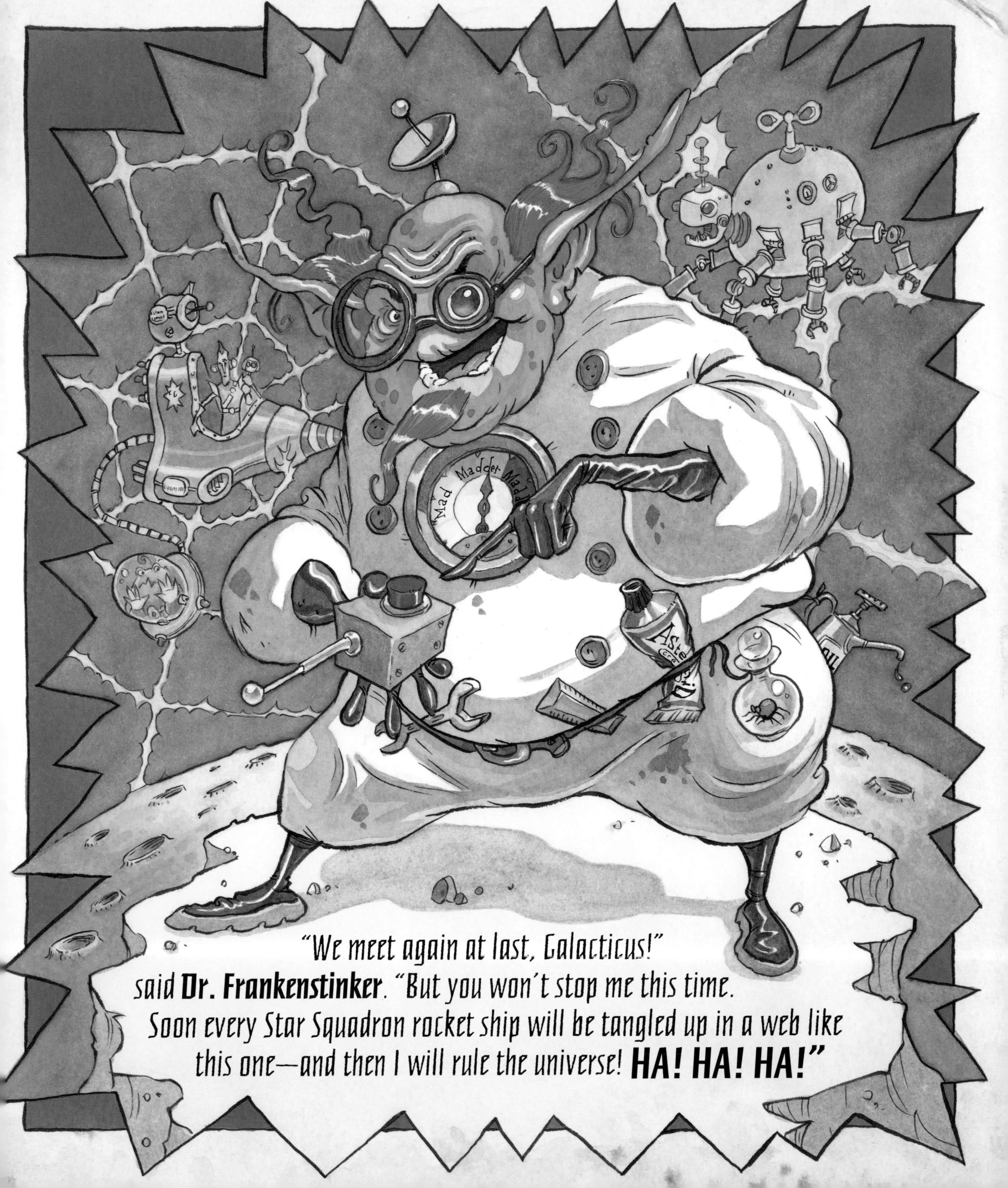
Mad
Madder

"We meet again at last, Galacticus!" said **Dr. Frankenstinker**. "But you won't stop me this time. Soon every Star Squadron rocket ship will be tangled up in a web like this one—and then I will rule the universe! **HA! HA! HA!**"

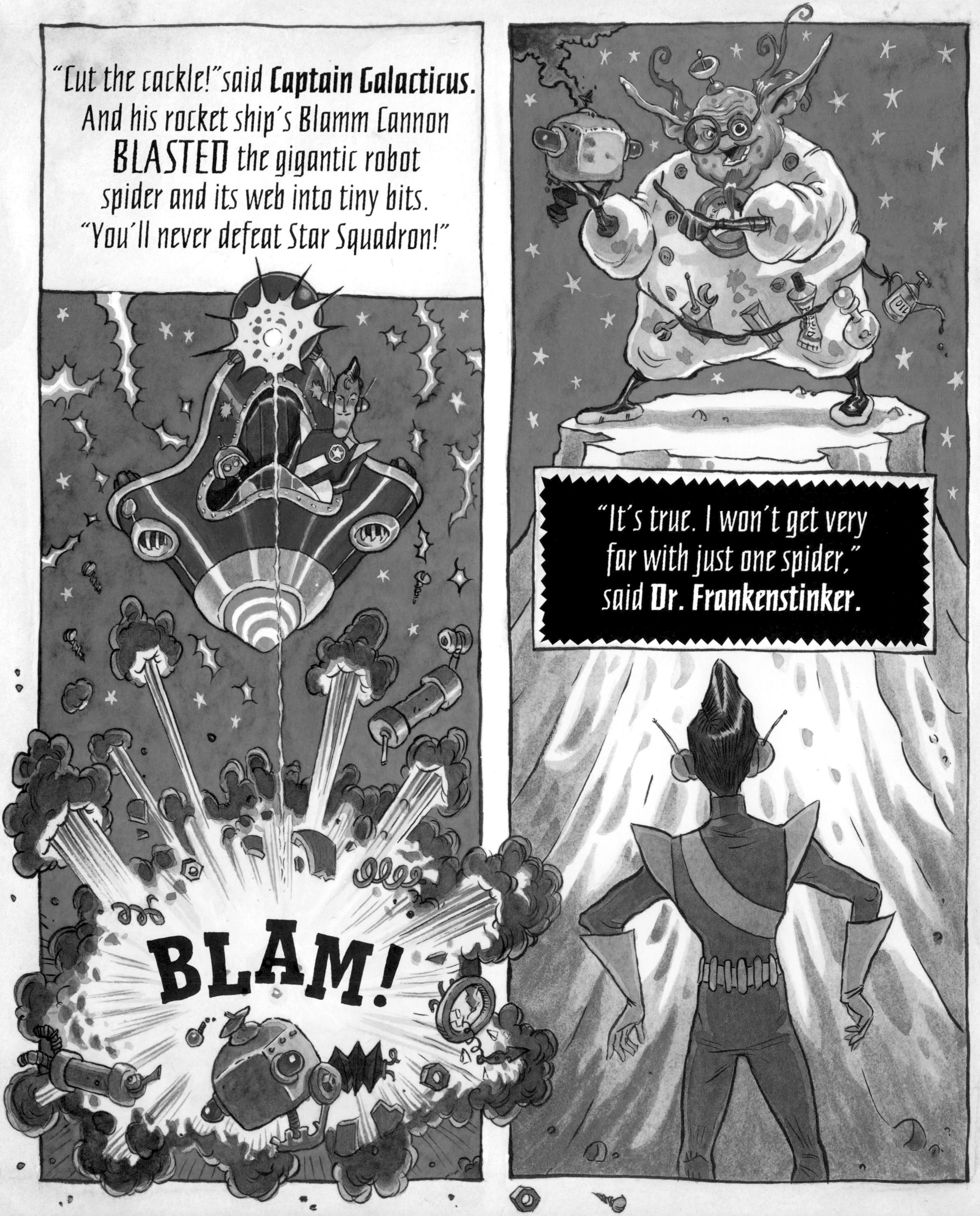
"Cut the cackle!" said **Captain Galacticus.** And his rocket ship's Blamm Cannon BLASTED the gigantic robot spider and its web into tiny bits. "You'll never defeat Star Squadron!"
BLAM!
"It's true. I won't get very far with just one spider," said **Dr. Frankenstinker.**

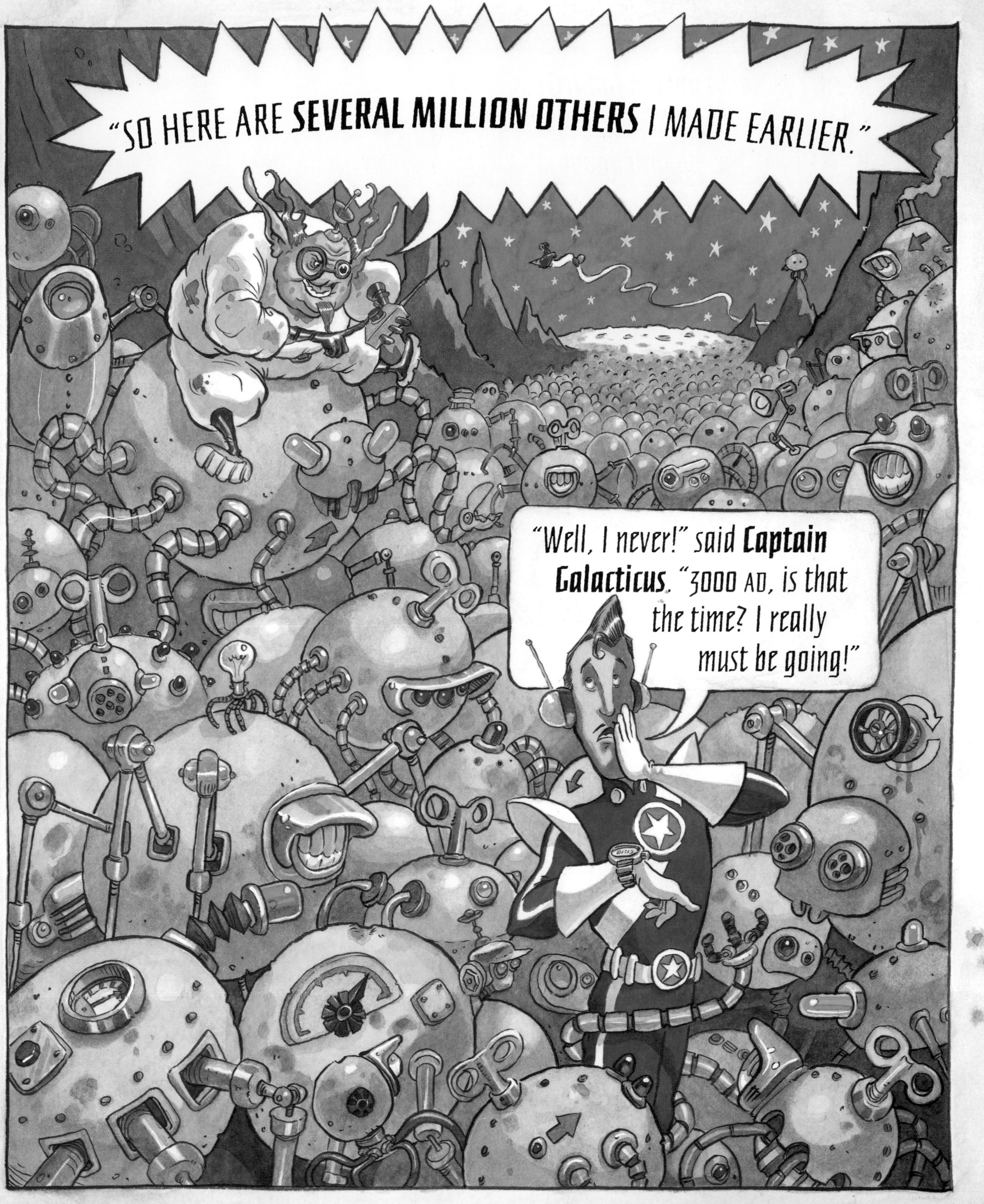
"SO HERE ARE **SEVERAL MILLION OTHERS** I MADE EARLIER."
"Well, I never!" said **Captain Galacticus**. "3000 AD, is that the time? I really must be going!"

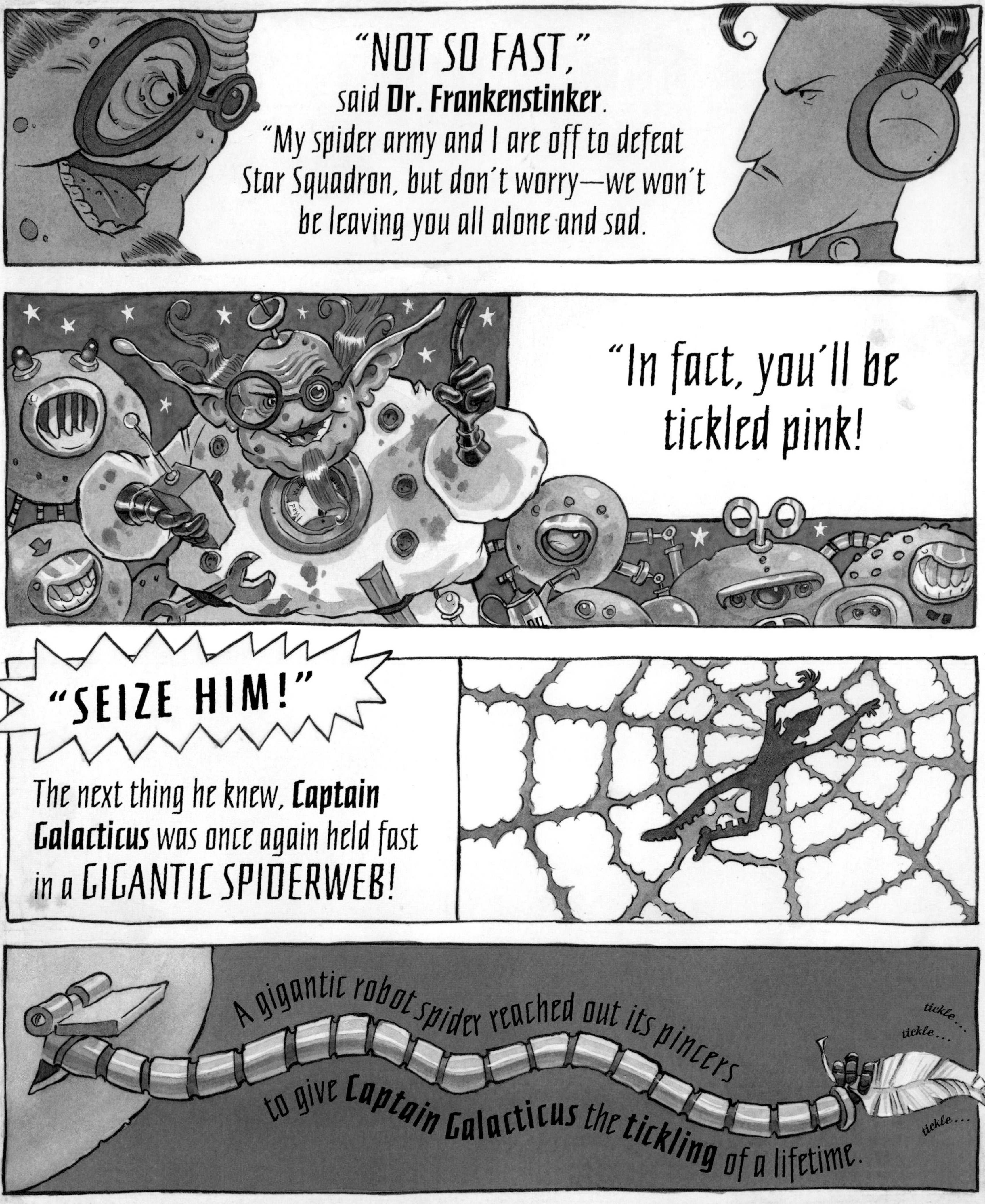
"NOT SO FAST,"
said **Dr. Frankenstinker**.
"My spider army and I are off to defeat Star Squadron, but don't worry—we won't be leaving you all alone and sad.
"In fact, you'll be tickled pink!
"SEIZE HIM!"
The next thing he knew, **Captain Galacticus** was once again held fast in a GIGANTIC SPIDERWEB!
A gigantic robot spider reached out its pincers to give **Captain Galacticus** the **tickling** of a lifetime.
tickle...
tickle...
tickle...

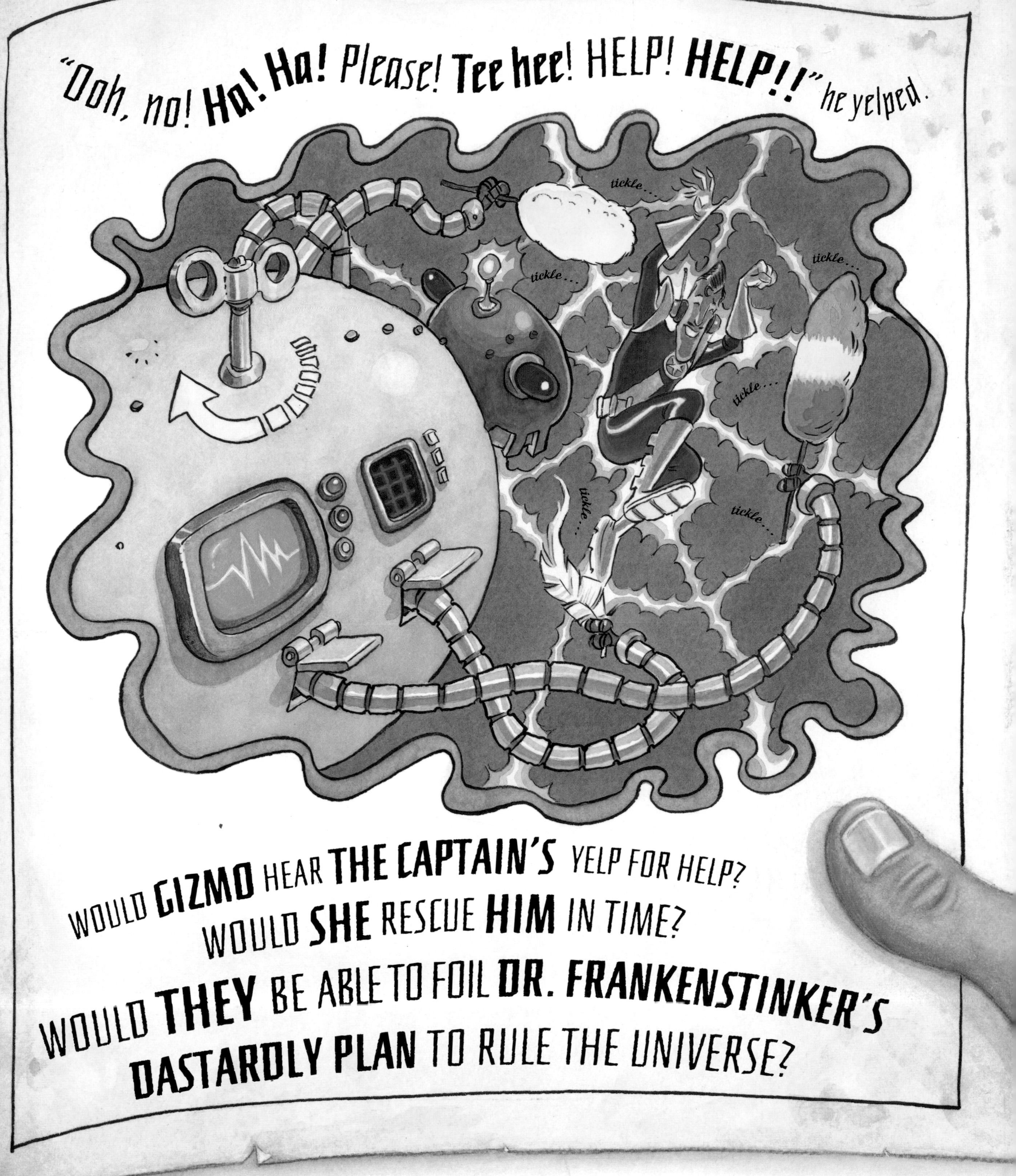
"Ooh, no! Ha! Ha! Please! Tee hee! HELP! HELP!!" he yelped.
tickle...
tickle...
tickle...
tickle...
tickle...
tickle...
WOULD GIZMO HEAR THE CAPTAIN'S YELP FOR HELP?
WOULD SHE RESCUE HIM IN TIME?
WOULD THEY BE ABLE TO FOIL DR. FRANKENSTINKER'S
DASTARDLY PLAN TO RULE THE UNIVERSE?

Mungo couldn't wait to find out. **But . . .**

THE
LAST PAGE
WAS
MISSING!

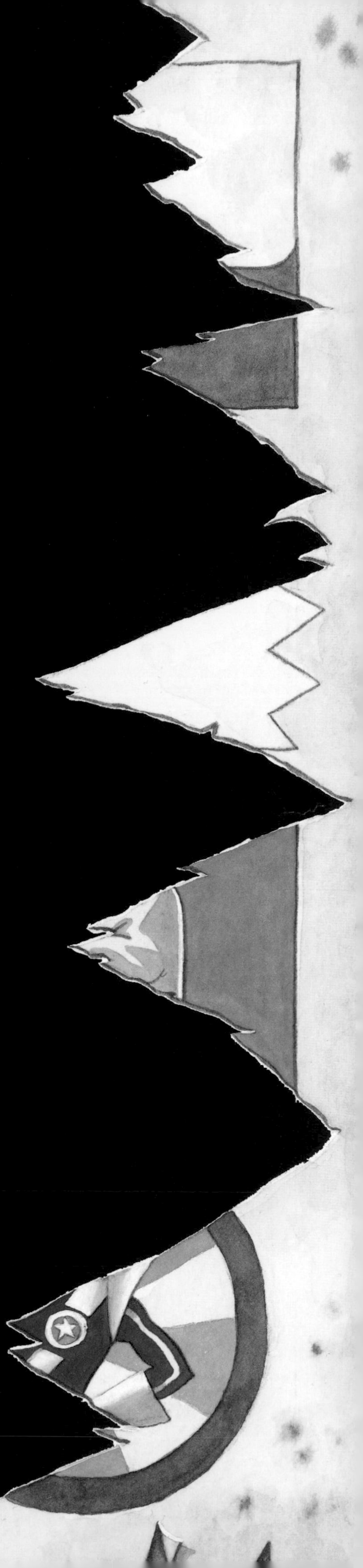

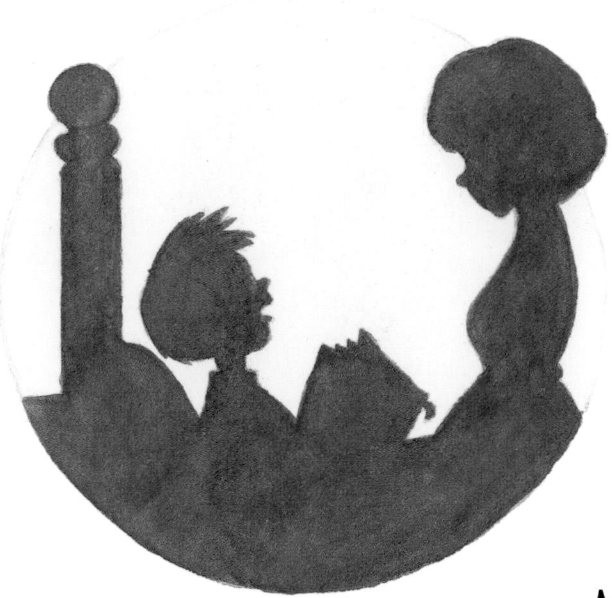

"But, Mom!" said Mungo.
"What happens next?"

"I don't know, darling,"
she said. "Why don't you
make up an ending?"
And she left him alone
with the book.

Make up an ending?
thought Mungo. I can't
make up an ending!

And then something
odd happened.

As he sat staring
at the cover, one
of the stars . . .

started to get *bigger.*

And bigger.

And bigger.

UNTIL . . .

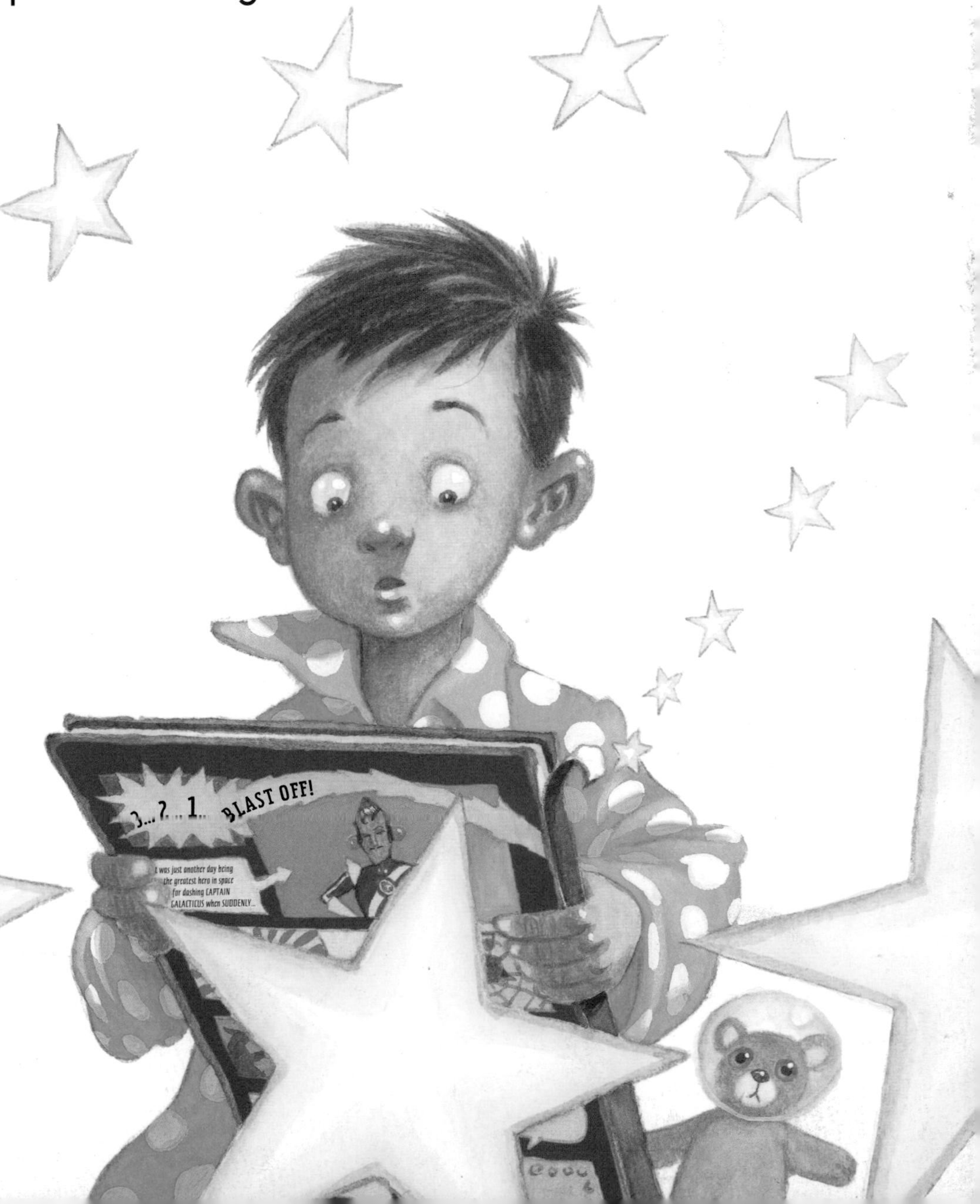
3... 2... 1... BLAST OFF!
was just another day being
the greatest hero in space
for dashing CAPTAIN
GALACTICUS when SUDDENLY...

With a

BOOM!

and a

Zoom!

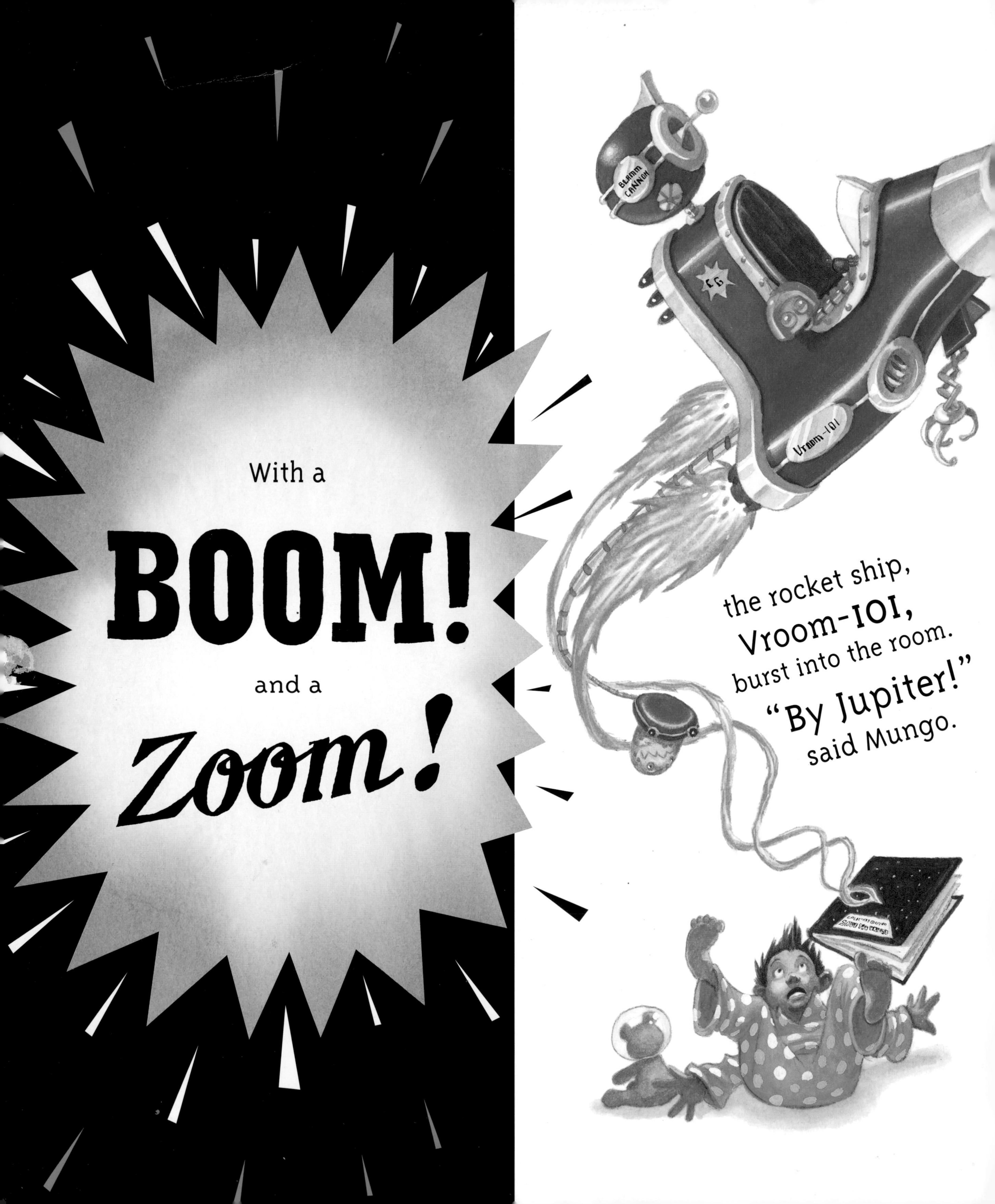
BLAMM CANNON
CG
Vroom-101

the rocket ship,
Vroom-101,
burst into the room.
"By Jupiter!"
said Mungo.

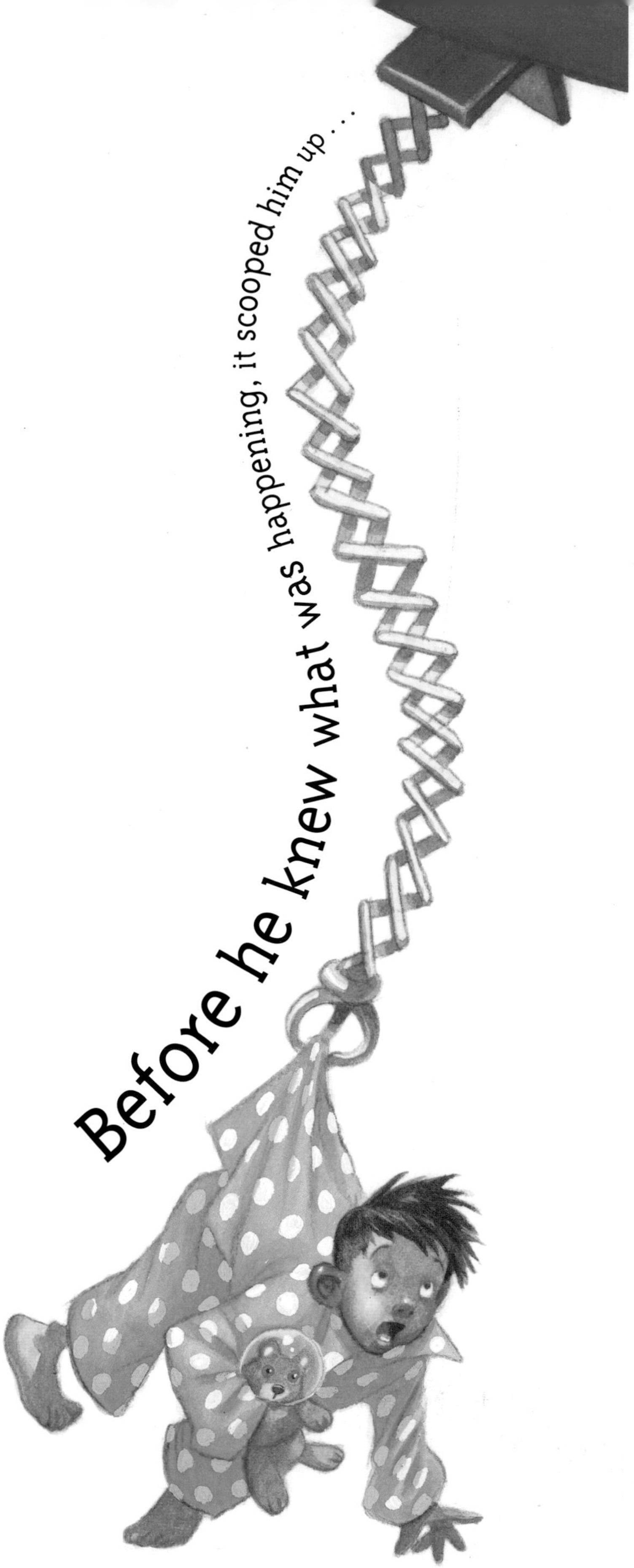

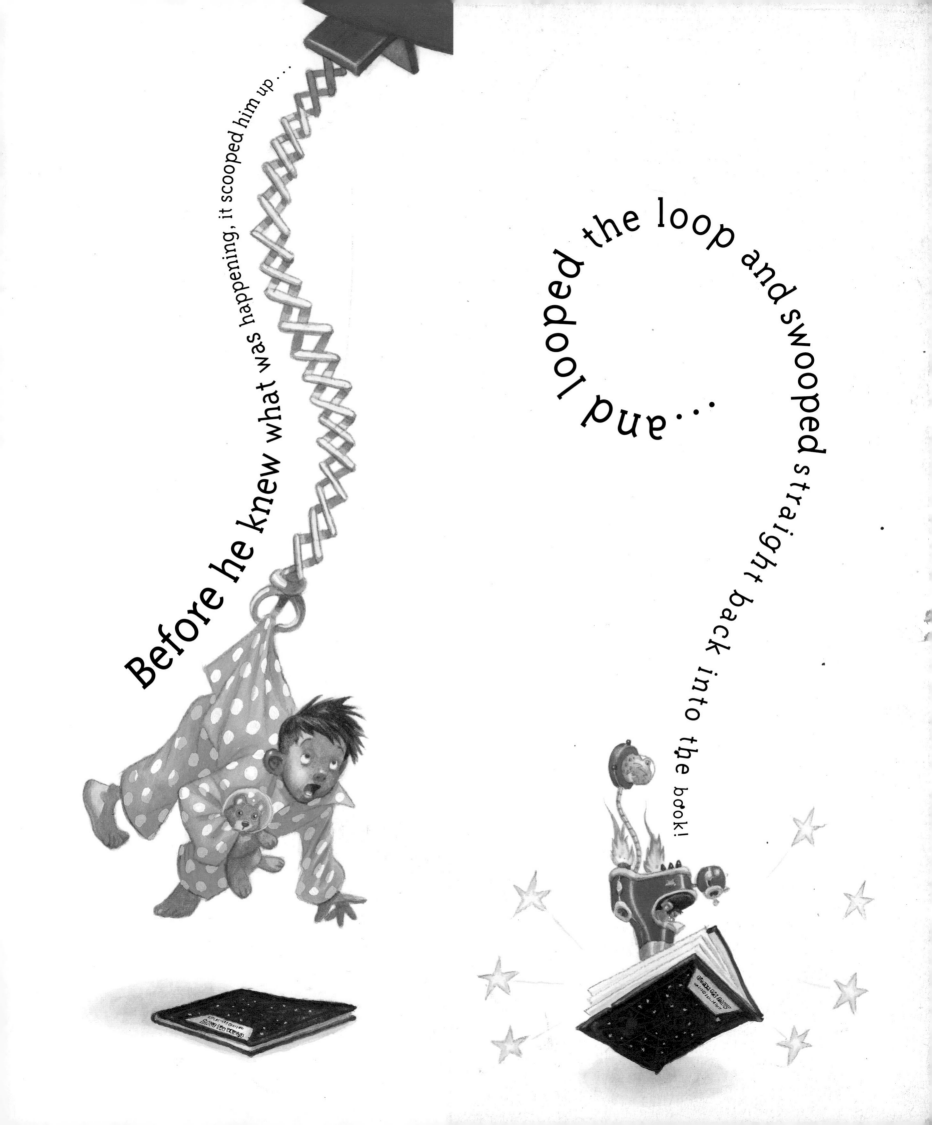

Before he knew what was happening, it scooped him up . . .

. . . and looped the loop and swooped straight back into the book!

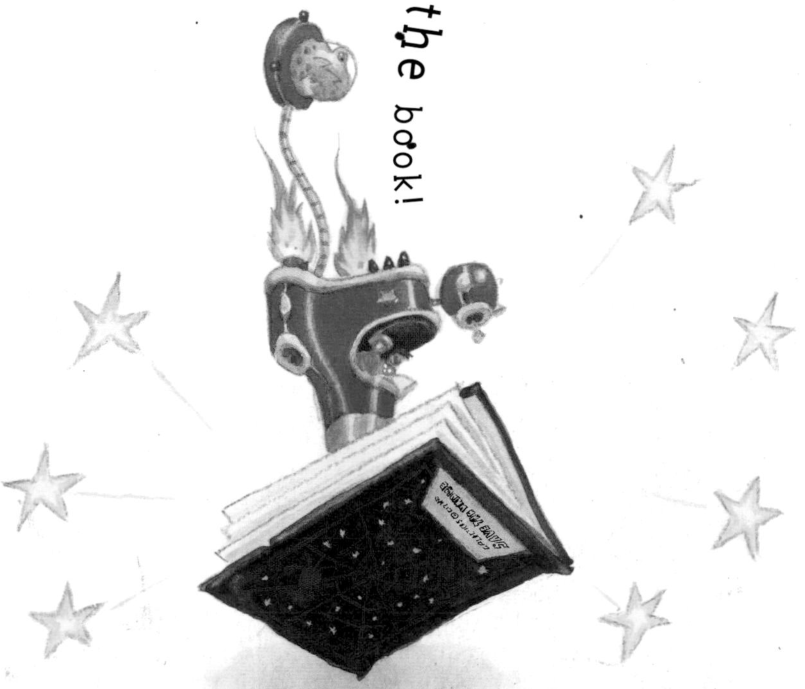

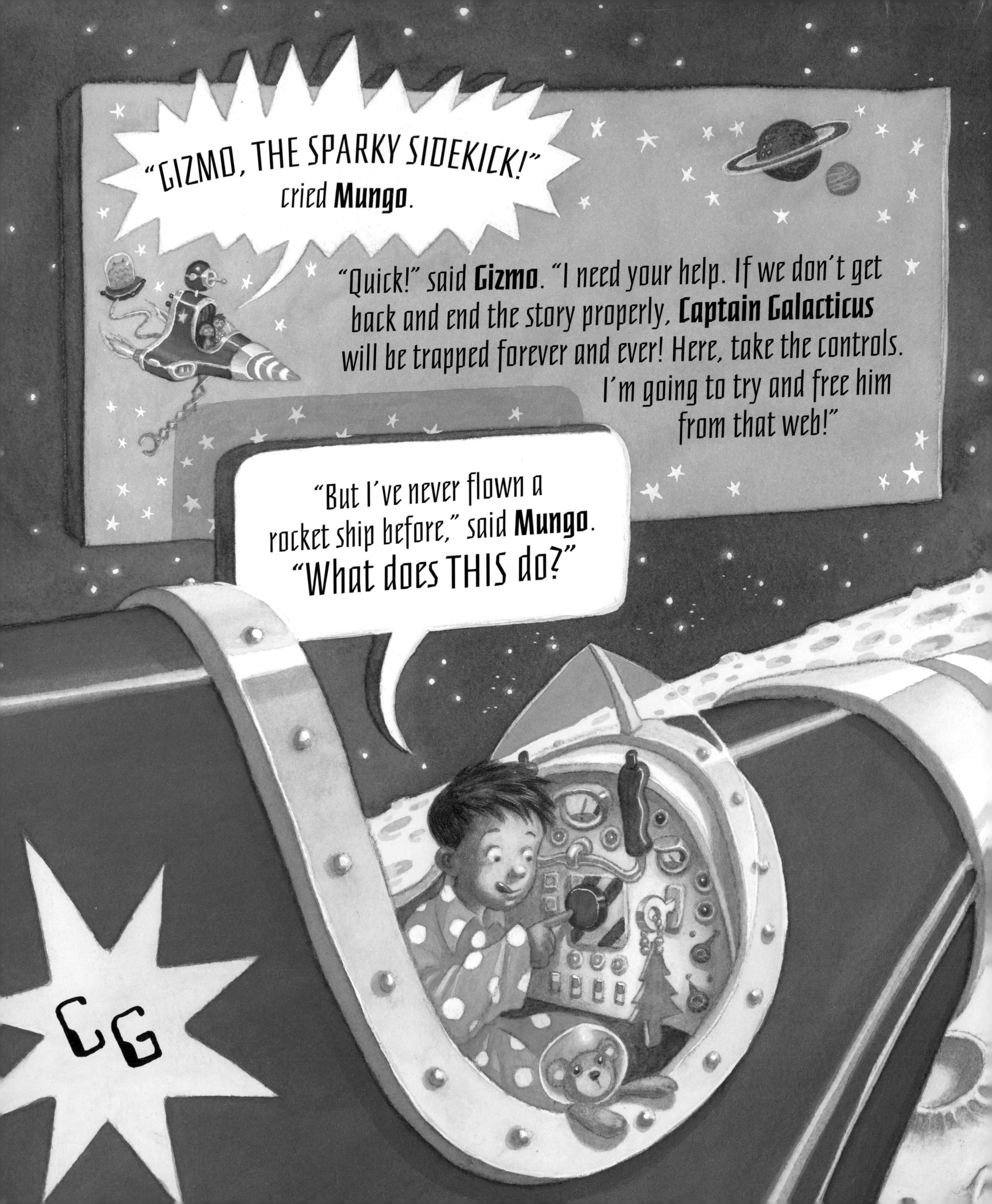
"GIZMO, THE SPARKY SIDEKICK!" cried **Mungo**.
"Quick!" said **Gizmo**. "I need your help. If we don't get back and end the story properly, **Captain Galacticus** will be trapped forever and ever! Here, take the controls. I'm going to try and free him from that web!"
"But I've never flown a rocket ship before," said **Mungo**. "What does THIS do?"
CG

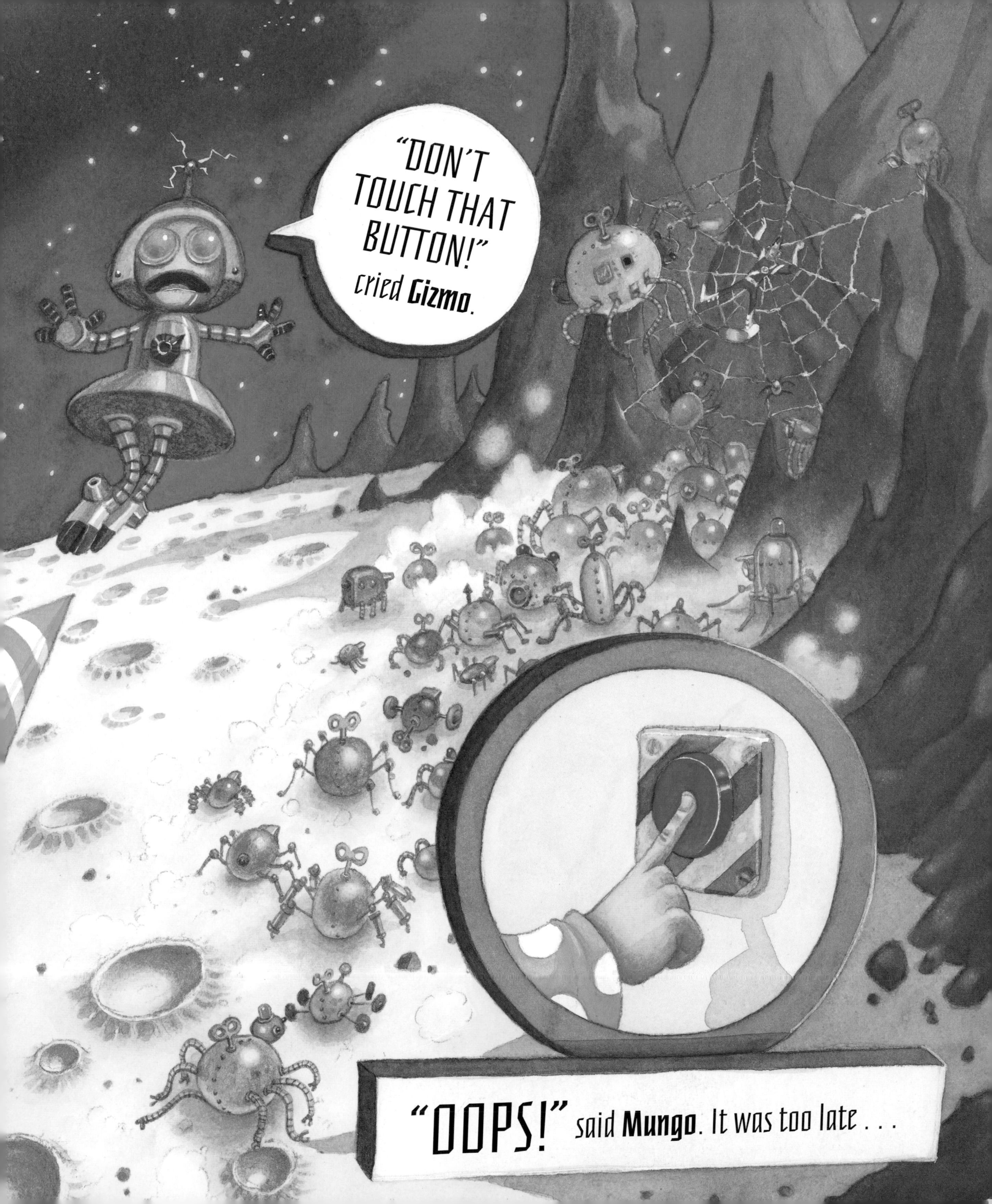
"DON'T TOUCH THAT BUTTON!" cried **Gizmo**.

"OOPS!" said **Mungo**. It was too late . . .

. . . everyone had forgotten the **GNASHING, SLASHING GOBBLEBEAST** on his way to space prison.

And now he was free and very, very hungry.

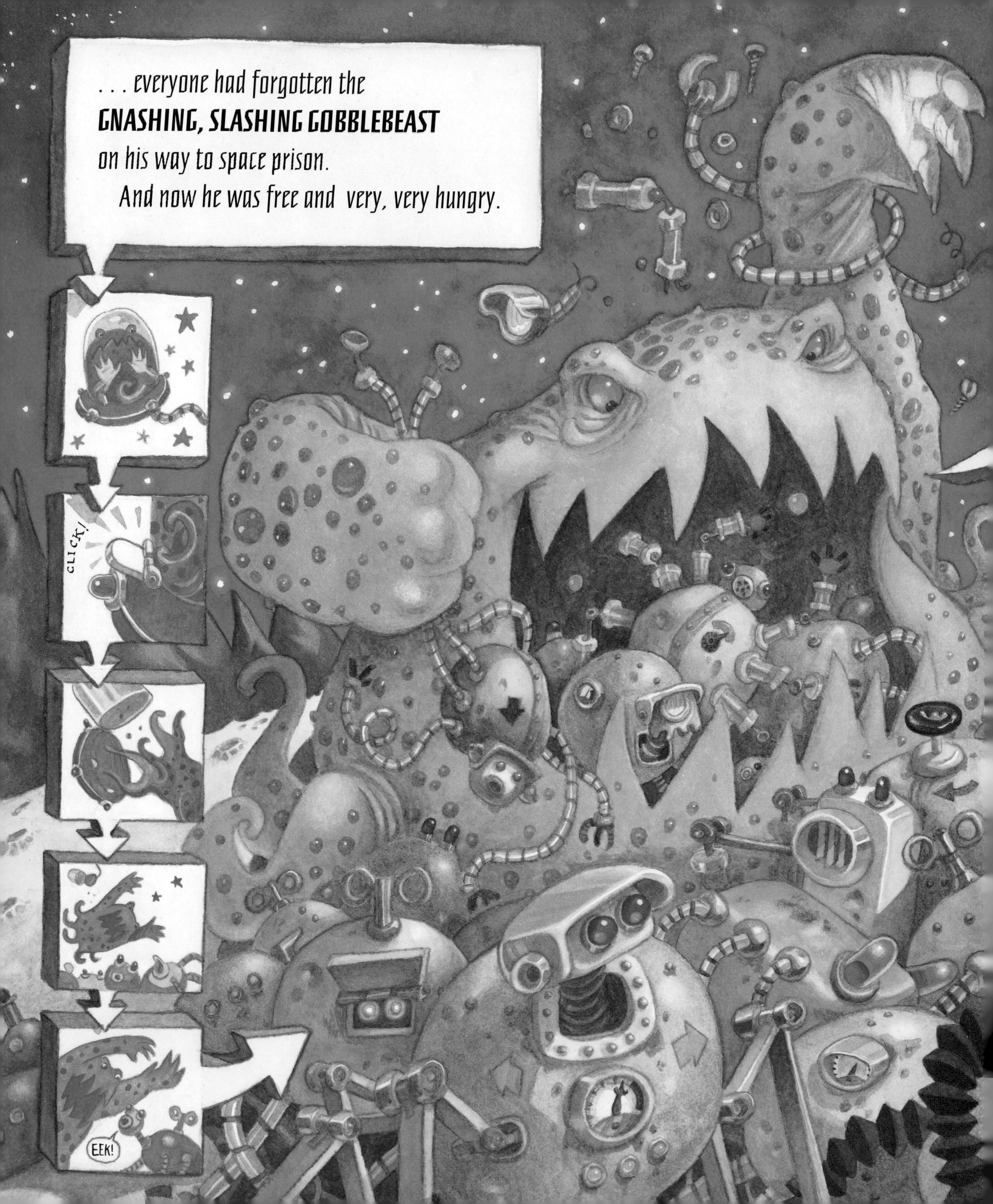
CLICK!
EEK!

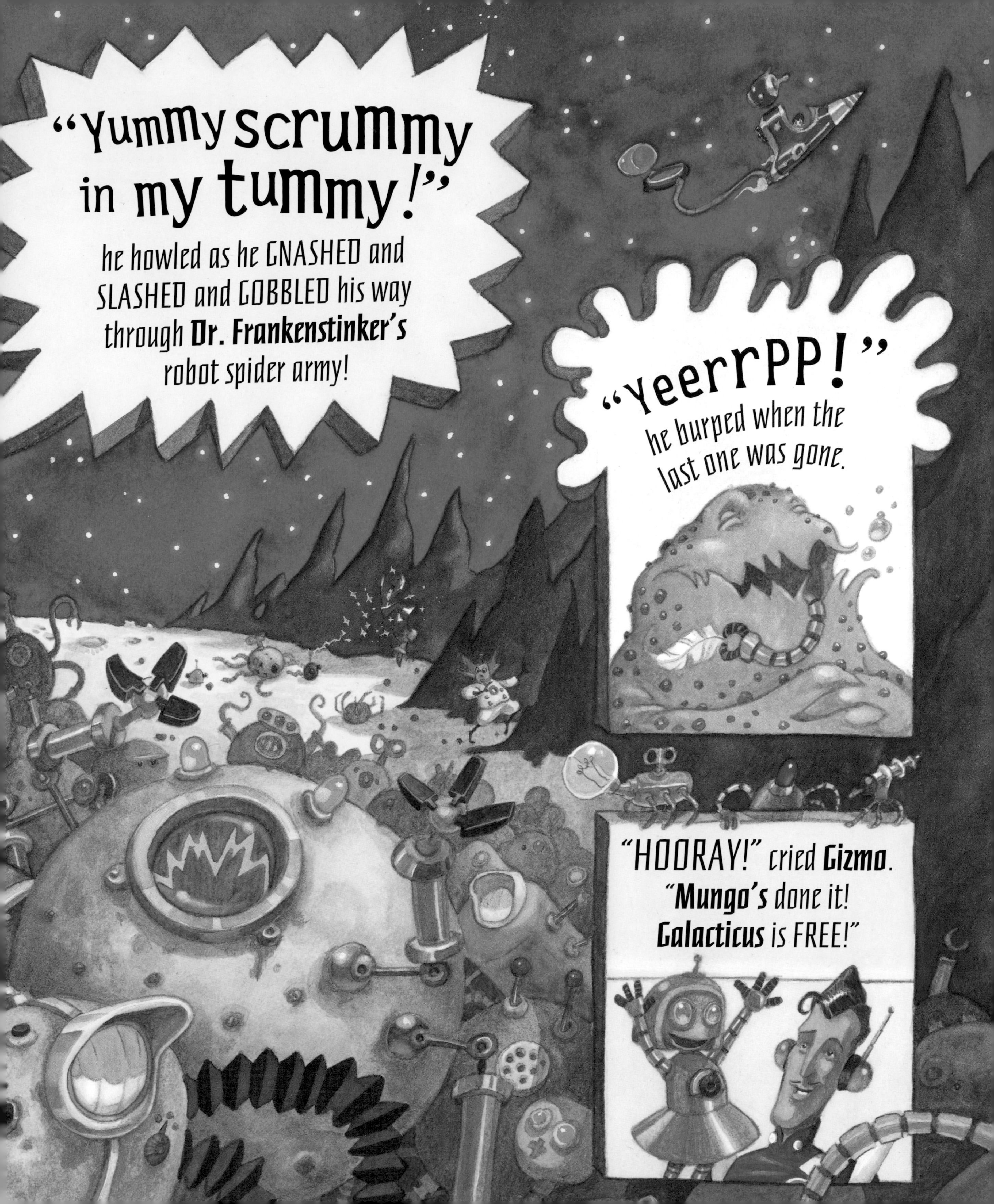
"Yummy scrummy in my tummy!"
he howled as he GNASHED and SLASHED and GOBBLED his way through **Dr. Frankenstinker's** robot spider army!
"YeerrPP!"
he burped when the last one was gone.
"HOORAY!" cried **Gizmo**. "**Mungo's** done it! **Galacticus** is FREE!"

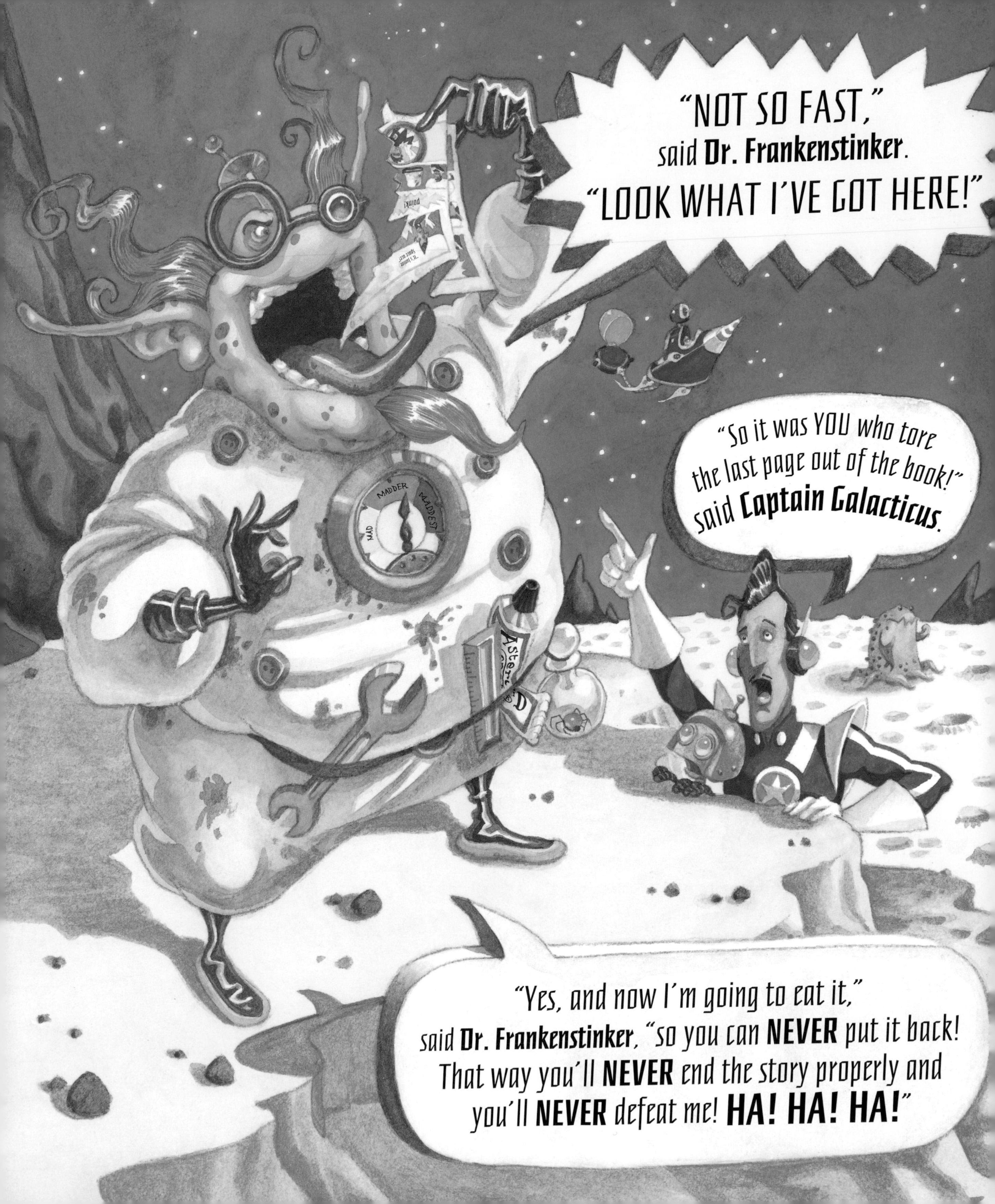
"NOT SO FAST," said **Dr. Frankenstinker**. "LOOK WHAT I'VE GOT HERE!"
"So it was YOU who tore the last page out of the book!" said **Captain Galacticus**.
MAD
MADDER
MADDEST
"Yes, and now I'm going to eat it," said **Dr. Frankenstinker**, "so you can **NEVER** put it back! That way you'll **NEVER** end the story properly and you'll **NEVER** defeat me! **HA! HA! HA!**"

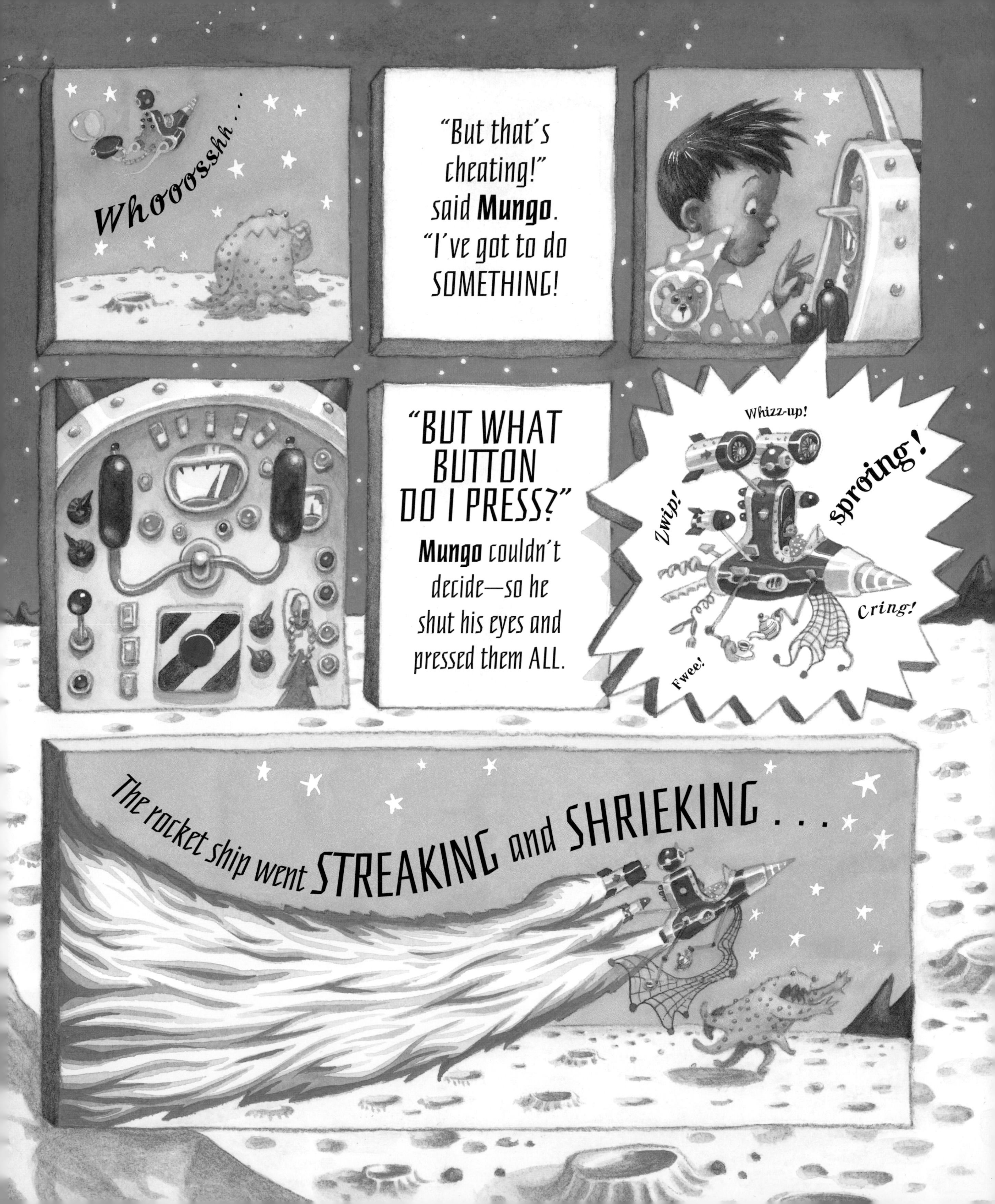
Whoooosshh . . .
"But that's cheating!" said Mungo. "I've got to do SOMETHING!
"BUT WHAT BUTTON DO I PRESS?"
Mungo couldn't decide—so he shut his eyes and pressed them ALL.
Whizz-up!
Zwip!
sproing!
Cring!
Fwee!
The rocket ship went STREAKING and SHRIEKING . . .

and **poinked** Dr. Frankenstinker IN THE **BOTTOM.**

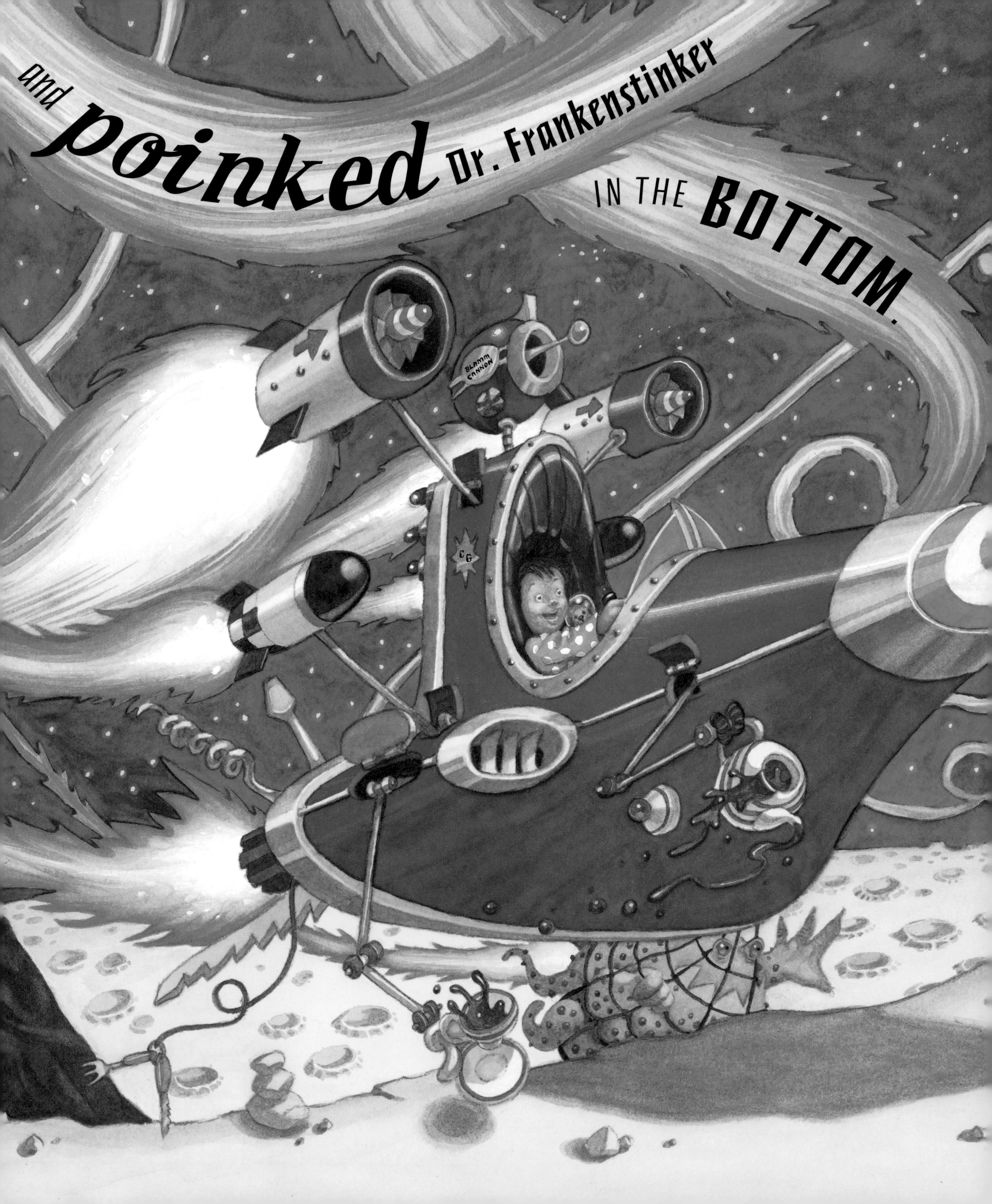
BLAMM CANNON
CG

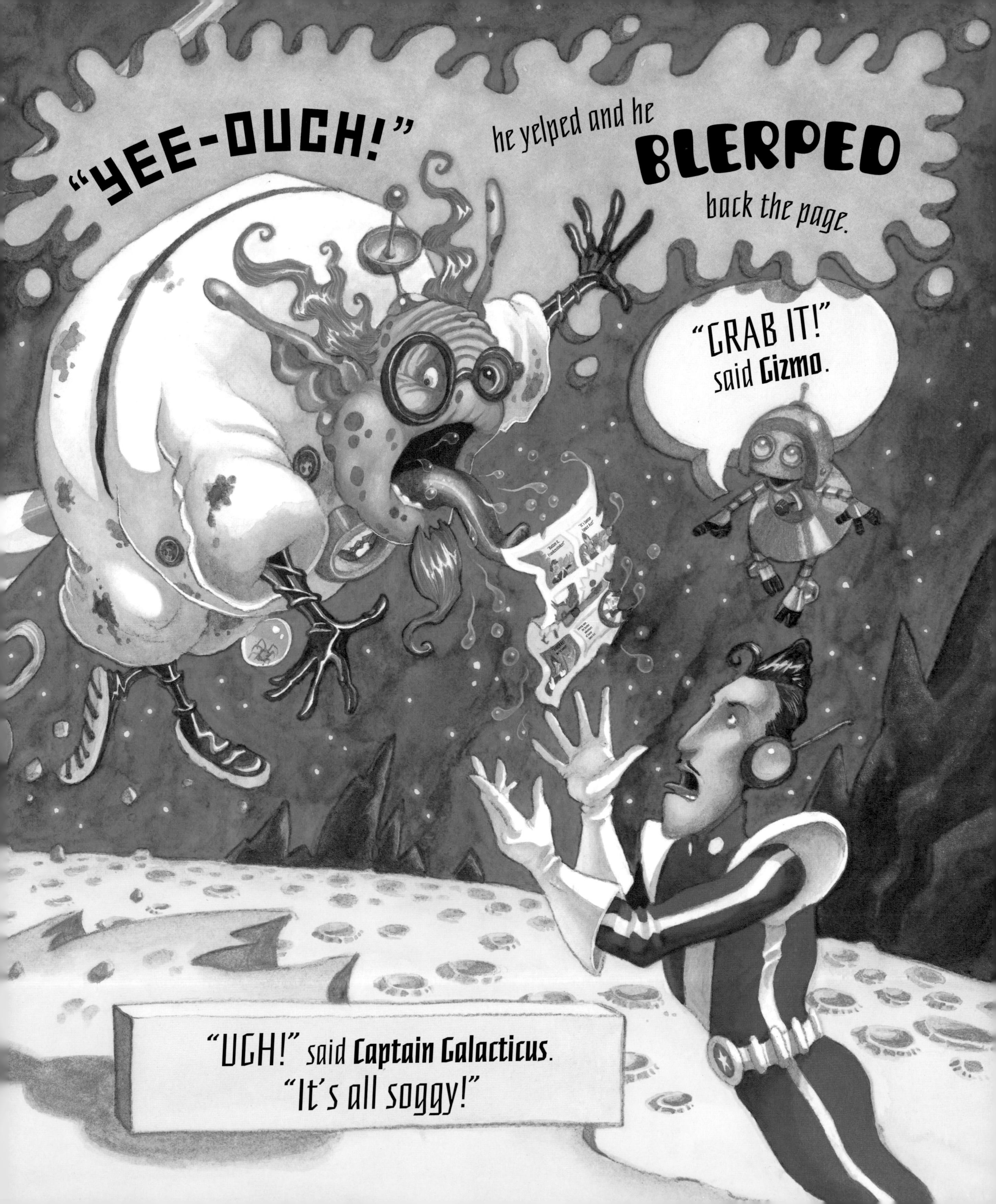
"YEE-OUCH!" he yelped and he BLERPED back the page.
"GRAB IT!" said Gizmo.
"UGH!" said Captain Galacticus. "It's all soggy!"

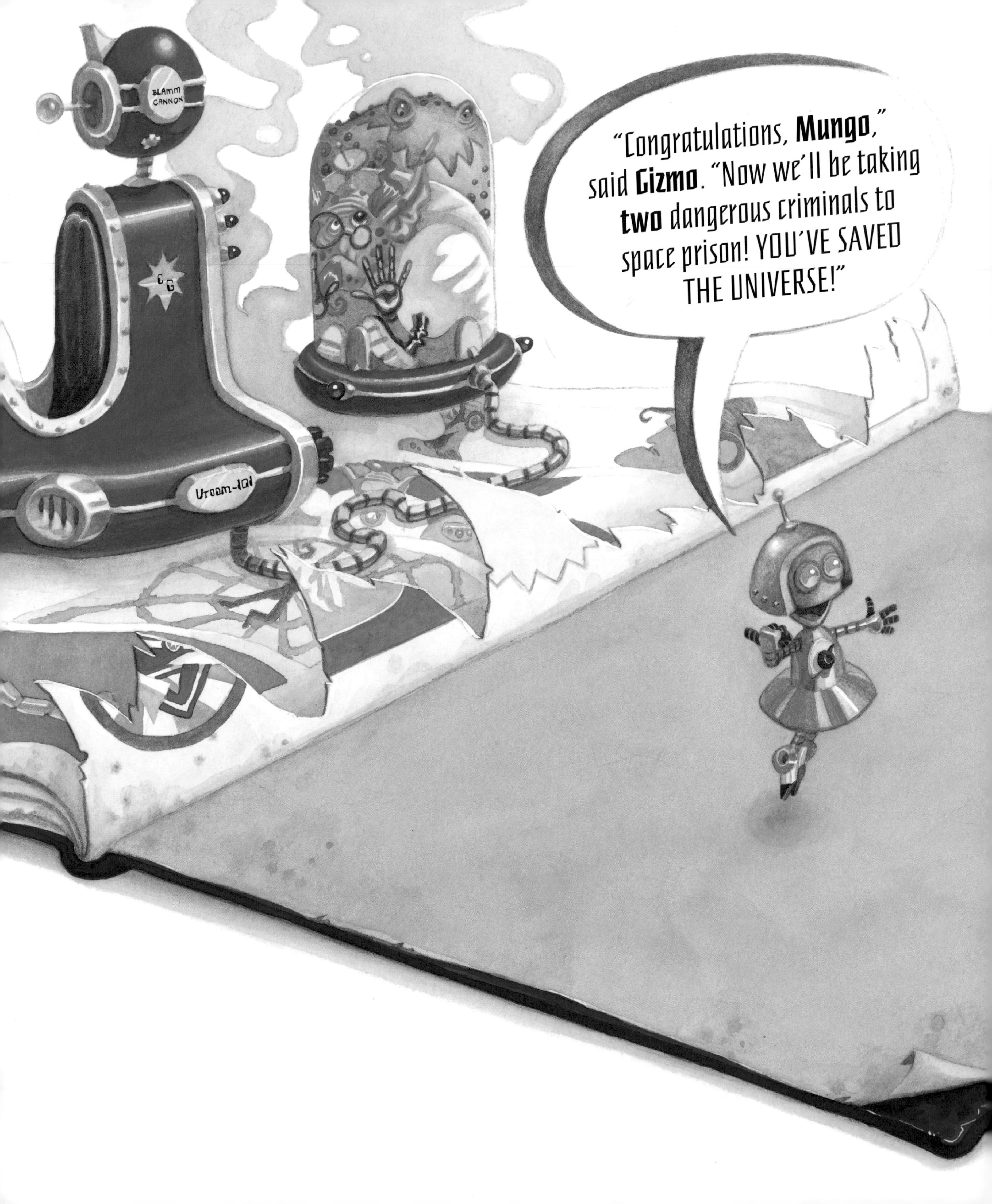
BLAMM CANNON
CG
Vroom-101
"Congratulations, **Mungo**," said **Gizmo**. "Now we'll be taking **two** dangerous criminals to space prison! YOU'VE SAVED THE UNIVERSE!"

"And, better still, you've given us a proper ending!" said **Captain Galacticus**.

"Take the last page—you can tape it back into the book, then **Dr. Frankenstinker** will never get his hands on it again!"

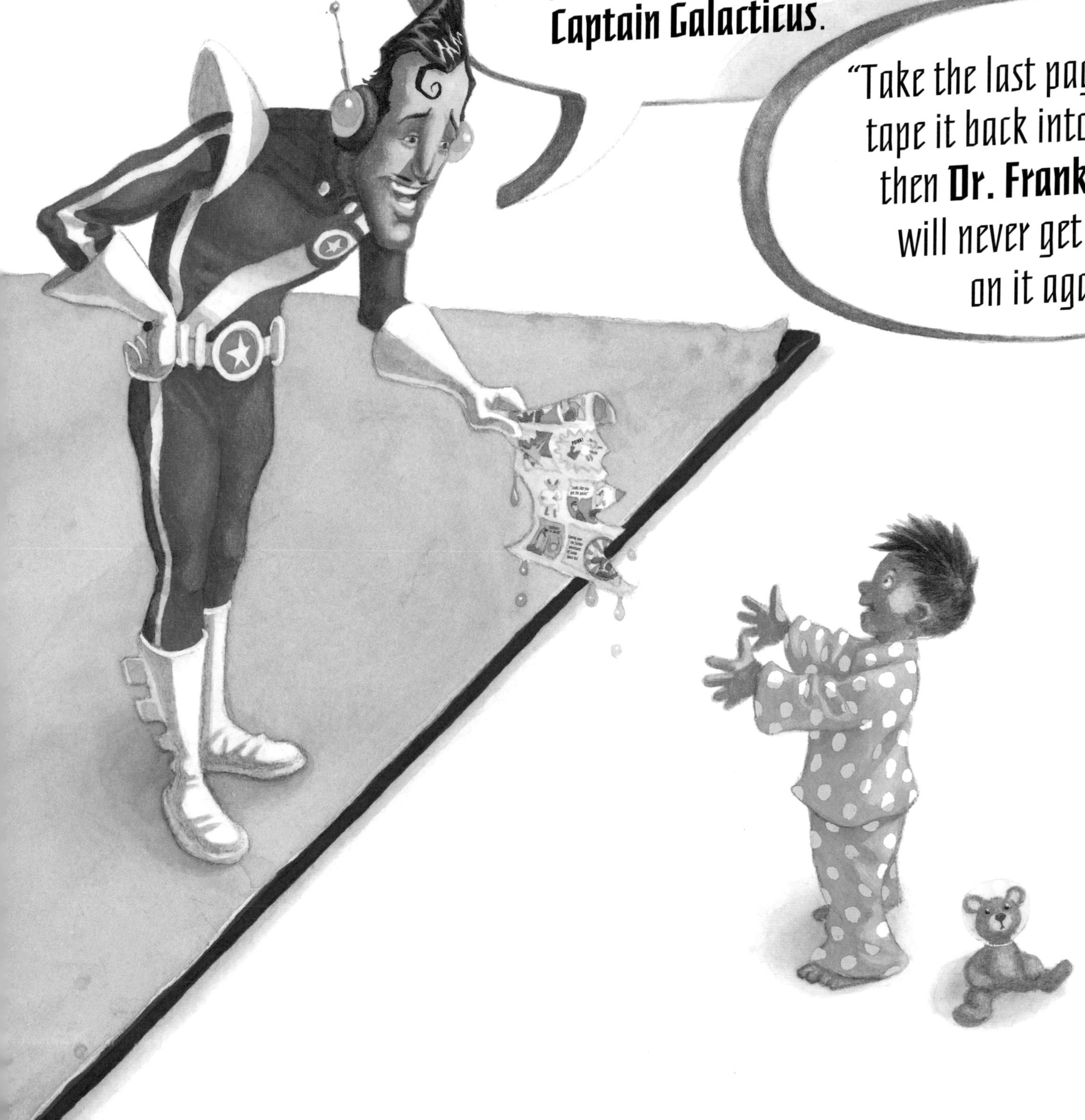

When Mungo's mom came back to turn off the light, Mungo was fast asleep. He was still clutching the last page of the book in which Captain Galacticus was rescued and the universe was saved by a mysterious stranger . . .

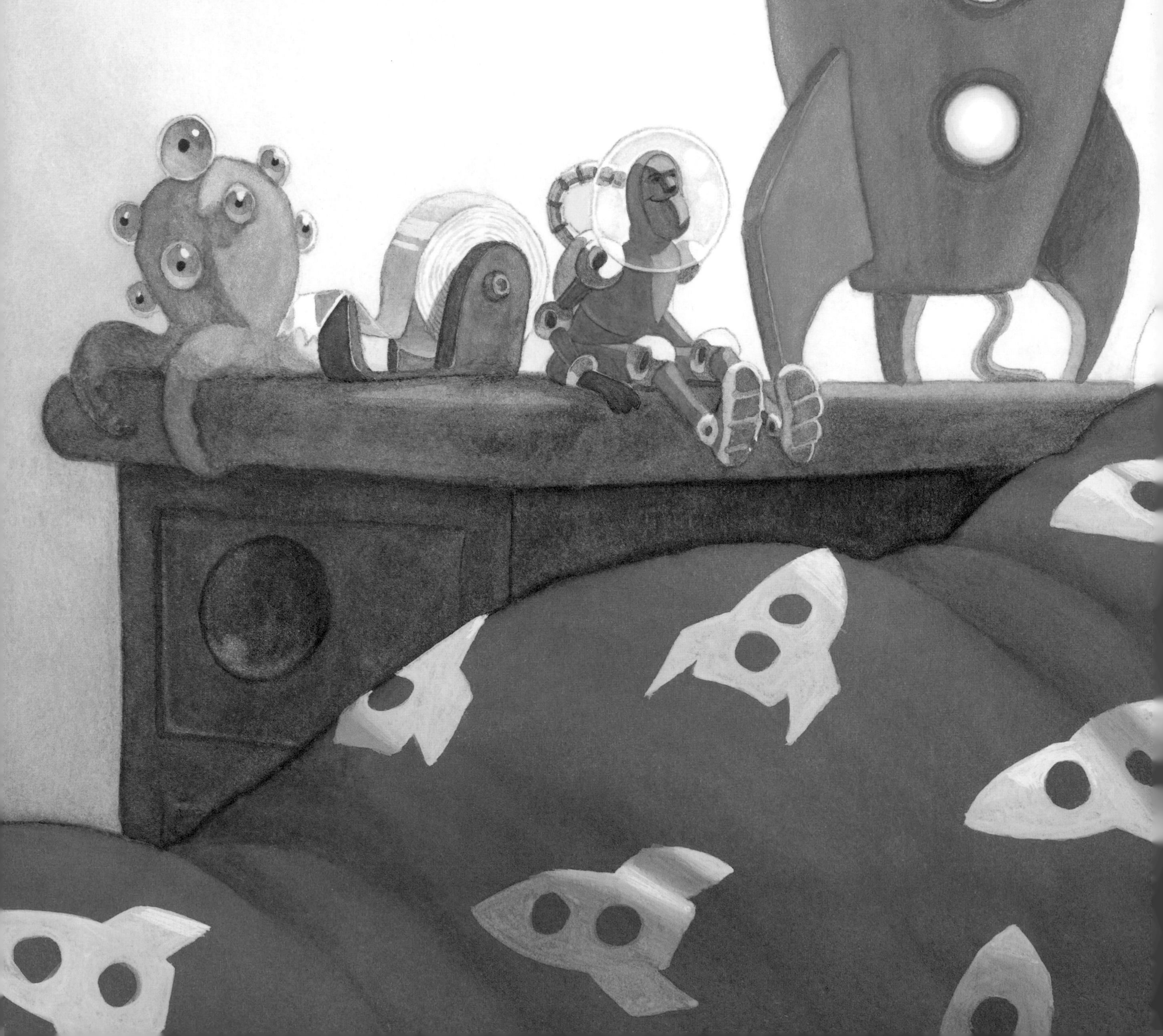

. . . the youngest ever member of Star Squadron.

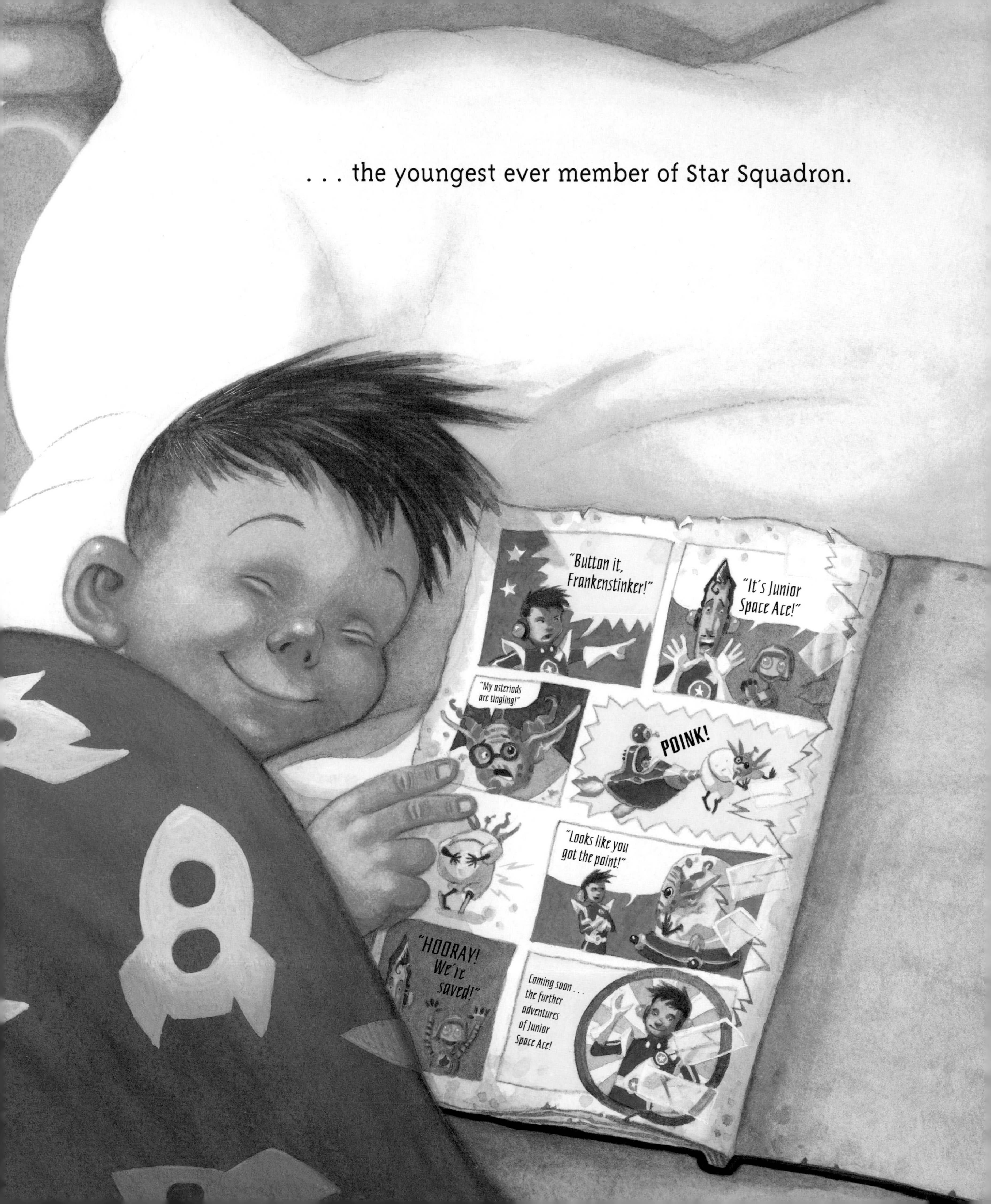

To James and Rowan, heroes of Star Squadron, with love—T.K.

For Matt and Anne, with love—A.S.

DIAL BOOKS FOR YOUNG READERS
A division of Penguin Young Readers Group
Published by The Penguin Group
Penguin Group (USA) Inc., 375 Hudson Street, New York, NY 10014, U.S.A.
Penguin Group (Canada), 90 Eglinton Avenue East, Suite 700, Toronto, Ontario, Canada M4P 2Y3 (a division of Pearson Penguin Canada Inc.)
Penguin Books Ltd, 80 Strand, London WC2R 0RL, England
Penguin Ireland, 25 St. Stephen's Green, Dublin 2, Ireland (a division of Penguin Books Ltd)
Penguin Group (Australia), 250 Camberwell Road, Camberwell, Victoria 3124, Australia (a division of Pearson Australia Group Pty Ltd)
Penguin Books India Pvt Ltd, 11 Community Centre, Panchsheel Park, New Delhi - 110 017, India
Penguin Group (NZ), 67 Apollo Drive, Rosedale, North Shore 0632, New Zealand (a division of Pearson New Zealand Ltd)
Penguin Books (South Africa) (Pty) Ltd, 24 Sturdee Avenue, Rosebank, Johannesburg 2196, South Africa
Penguin Books Ltd, Registered Offices: 80 Strand, London WC2R 0RL, England

First published in the United States 2008
by Dial Books for Young Readers
Published in Great Britain 2007
by Puffin Books

Text copyright © 2007 by Timothy Knapman
Pictures copyright © 2007 by Adam Stower

Printed in China
1 3 5 7 9 10 8 6 4 2

Library of Congress Cataloging-in-Publication Data avaiable upon request

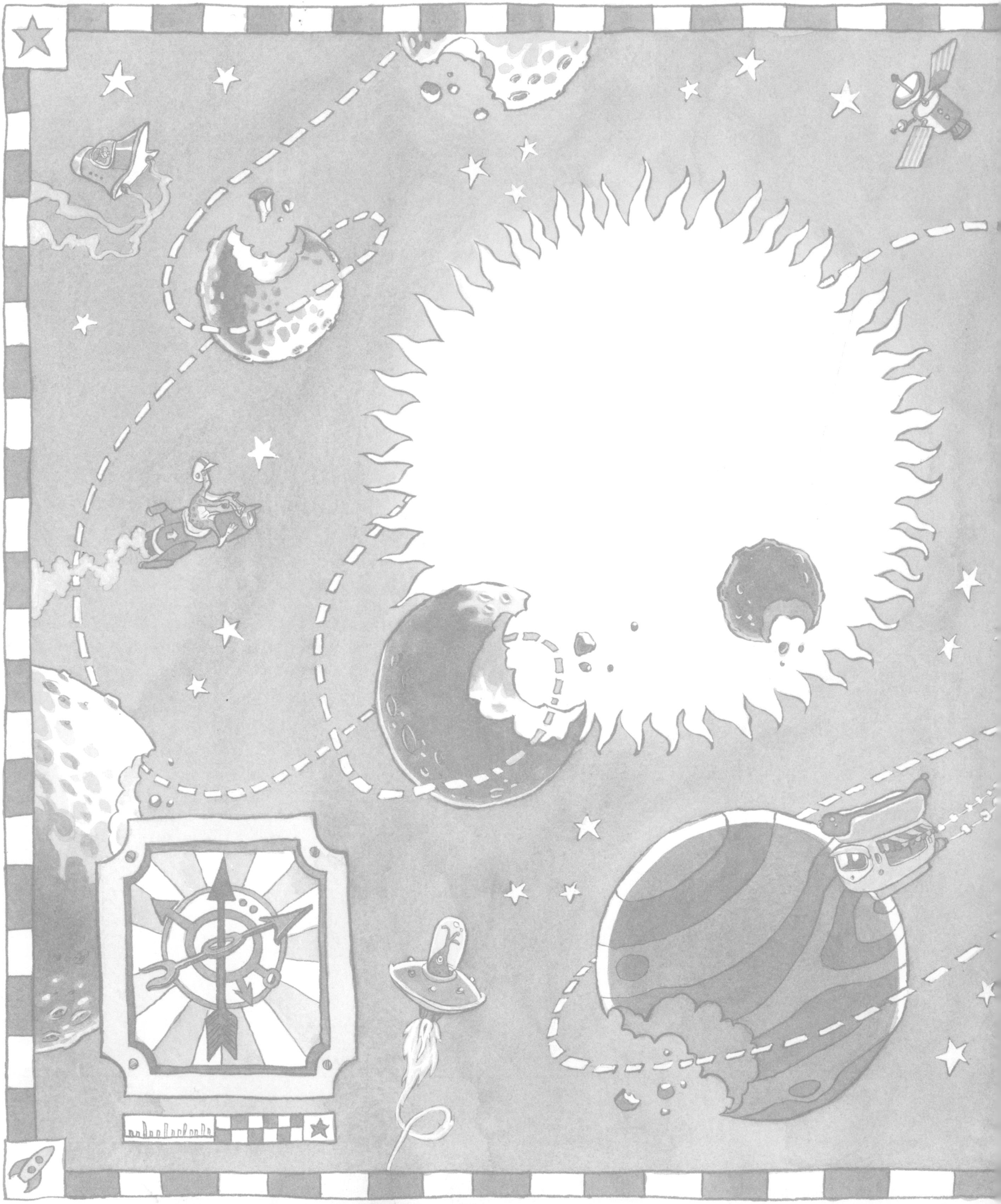